Enjoy this trip to Italy! Barbara Lohr

Her Favorite Honeymoon

by

Barbara Lohr

Purple Egret Press

Purple Egret Press
Savannah, Georgia 31411

Cover Art by Kim Killion – The Killion Group
Editing by Nicole Zoltack

Print ISBN: 978-0-9896023-5-8
Digital ISBN: 978-0-9896023-4-1

Dedication

for

Kelly & Shannon

May you have many adventures.

Also by Barbara Lohr

Windy City Romance
Her Favorite Mistake

New Adult Novellas
Summer of the Fireflies
The Salty Carmel Christmas

Chapter 1

The locker room reeked of teenage boys and wet towels. Amy's footsteps echoed on the white tile floor. Jason's office was just ahead, past the last row of metal lockers. She couldn't wait to tell him about the online special she'd scored for a luxury hotel in Venice. What a coup. Just thinking about their Tuscany honeymoon gave her shivers.

Jason always stayed late after football practice, mapping out new plays. Only three weeks until school started, right after they'd return from their honeymoon. Excitement revved up her pulse.

Amy popped her head in his door. Looked like a bomb had exploded. The light from Jason's desk lamp revealed scattered papers and discarded workout clothes, along with a spilled can of pop and some cheese curls. After snapping off the light—Glenn, their principal, always asked them to conserve energy—she rushed past.

Poor guy. Wasn't easy to teach history and coach football too. Back in the shower room, water was running. Clouds of warm steam beaded the walls and coated her skin. Reminded her of one of those sexy movies. Swiping the claw clip from her hair, she shook it out, smiling as caramel curls bounced over her shoulders.

She was scheduled for a cut and blonde highlights before the wedding.

Picturing Jason under a stream of hot water, she slipped out of her aqua T-shirt and sports bra. Kind of kinky, but they'd be alone. Wasn't this what a girl did for her future husband?

Husband. She liked it.

Another sound caught her attention. Amy grabbed an open locker, the metal biting into her palm. Pressing her clothes to a heart gone wild, she listened. Through the splash of the water, she heard deep, satisfied groans.

"Jason?" She rounded the corner. "Jason!"

Through the billowing steam, she could see them clearly— Greta Hanson, the phys ed teacher, and Jason, bodies slick and their position pretty creative. He'd never suggested it with her, that's for sure.

"Amy!" Jason's eyes widened.

With a tricky twist used by her cheerleaders, Greta flipped her head up, blonde hair fanning onto her shoulders. Usually, the queen of the Physical Education Department wore a blue warm-up suit as she swung through the hallways with long, sexy strides.

The blue suit didn't do her justice.

Amy froze. Was her heart still beating?

Looking annoyed, as if she'd been interrupted in a meeting, Greta gave Jason a pat on the shoulder and zipped past Amy, head high.

Feeling like she'd been struck by a hit-and-run driver, Amy thought she might faint. The shower room was unbearably warm, and she couldn't catch her breath.

Jason turned off the water, pipes squealing in protest. Jamming one hand through his wet hair, he smiled. "Hey, babe, I can explain."

"No, I don't think you can." Backing out, she groped the slick wall and stumbled smack into one of the benches.

"Amy, this is not what you think, trust me."

"I'm not blind, Jason." Amy rammed her head into her T-shirt, shoved her sports bra into her bag and ran for the door.

"Amy, hold on!"

When she pushed the metal doors open, she was blinded by the bright sunlight. Swiping at her eyes, she veered toward the Toyota, tore open the door, and flung herself into the hot interior. She had to pull over three times, but somehow she made it home.

But their apartment felt like a lie. Wedding gifts piled in the living room. Lists trailing from the refrigerator. Her wedding gown hanging in the guest room closet. The subtle lines of the long organza skirt, bell-shaped sleeves and delicately beaded bodice had fulfilled a life-long dream.

Two months of her teaching salary and she'd never wear it.

Sinking into the desk chair, Amy caught sight of herself in the mirror and whimpered. Her shirt was on backward and inside out. Hair straggled to her shoulders, and her bloodshot eyes looked like she'd been crying for days. She was a hot mess. The wedding had to be canceled...and the honeymoon too. Rapallo, Florence and Venice—she'd never see them.

Damn it. A hiccup shook her.

St. Basil's Church, the Stone Cold band, Elks Lodge, Missy's Fine Catering—they all had to be notified. And her family. What would her mother and Aunt Em say? Good grief, she needed help. Fumbling through her black tote, she grabbed her cell phone and called her younger sister. "Caitlin, the wedding's off."

"What did you say? Why?"

"Don't feel bad. Really, it's for the best."

"Thank God." Her sister sighed.

"What?"

"He was never good enough for you."

The sharp intake of air stung Amy's throat, raw from crying. "When were you going to tell me?"

"You seemed so happy." Caitlin hesitated. "I'm glad you snapped out of it before you tied yourself to that dead weight, as in 'till death do us part."

"Not like I had a choice, Cait." She described the ugly scene in the shower room.

"Greta? You mean that horsey-looking phys ed teacher?"

"That would be the one. Trust me, without clothes, not so horsey."

"What about the honeymoon?"

"I'll never… get my… money back," Amy moaned through her hiccups.

"Go anyway. Have a great time."

"Right. Alone. What fun would that be?"

"Wish I could go, but the shop's so busy. End of summer sales and all." Amy could almost hear the wheels turning in her sister's head.

"Don't even think about it." One week of her sister's pity? Rather stick a pin in her eye.

"Listen, I've heard about this website called Travel Chums. It matches you up for trips if you're solo."

Amy snorted. "Who could leave in two weeks?"

"Maybe another teacher who wants a final fling before she hits the books again?"

A woman who doesn't know me, who doesn't know how stupid I've been. "What if we don't get along?"

"Two women who like art museums? Put that in your profile. You can't miss. Of course you'll get along."

Of the two of them, Caitlin was the feisty sister—the one who didn't know what to do after graduation so she opened her own T-shirt shop. Everything always worked out for Caitlin. Amy had to plan and schedule to make life happen. She was the teacher who had her grades in the day before they were due.

So damn depressing.

She expelled a long breath. "Mom and Aunt Em will be so disappointed. Those expensive new dresses they bought for the wedding? I can't face them."

"I'll take care of everything. Work on your trip. Travel Chums," Caitlin threw out again before hanging up.

One clean sweep of her arm and Jason's sport magazines toppled off the desk. Amy grabbed her laptop. When the latch wouldn't open, she nearly threw it across the room. Instead, she dropped her head into her hands and sobbed until all she had left was a thin string of hiccups.

How could this have happened?

"*Travel Chums*?" Mallory Thornton stared at the computer screen. Was this his cousin's idea of a joke? The conference room of the Oglethorpe Club echoed with the clicking of Chad's mouse. Almost midnight. The two cousins might be the only people left in the private club.

Chad rocked back in his chair, and his devilish smile didn't bode well. "Heard a client talking about this site. Had a great time with a woman who was a history professor. Might get you out of your slump—a bright, intelligent woman who knows how to have fun."

"Land sakes. You really know how to hurt a guy."

Glancing at Mallory over one shoulder, Chad frowned. "It's been eight months since the divorce. All you do is work. That's no life."

Chad might have a point.

A woman stared back at Mallory from the screen, darkish hair yanked into a tight knot. Granny glasses perched on her nose. Not much to look at except for her shy smile.

He took another sip of his Maker's Mark. "So it's come to this?"

"Afraid so." Chad scrolled through the bio. "We could check out dating sites, but that doesn't seem to be the problem. You could have a date every night right here in Savannah."

Mallory groaned. "My word, every woman in the city wants an escort for some gala."

"So they say. What they really want is you, my man. Word's out about your divorce, and the hunt is on. A trip to someplace new with a woman you don't know might be just the thing to fire your engines. Someone who doesn't know Thornton Enterprises."

"Well, not *that* woman." Mallory jabbed a finger at the screen.

"Fine." One click and she was gone. Chad hopped onto another site. "But after Rhonda Reynolds, I'll do the choosing. Just for this trip, anyway."

Following their weekly game of cards at the Oglethorpe Club, they'd stopped in one of the conference rooms. Chad liked to review daily figures from his import auto business. Instead, he'd gone on this site, an online service that matched up traveling singles. Mallory had to get his mind around that absurd idea.

As Chad continued clicking on websites for single travelers, exotic scenes faded in and out on the screen. White sand beaches stretching for miles. Stone castles perched on soaring cliffs. Art treasures housed in architectural wonders. Something stirred inside. Maybe he'd eaten one too many deep-fried hush puppies.

"Might be good to get away." He rubbed the back of his neck. Good God, he was tired of being fresh meat on the Savannah social scene. And after Hurricane Rhonda, as his cousin called Mallory's ex-wife, he didn't trust his judgment.

One more click of that damn mouse and Chad had flipped back to the original site. Travel Chums?

Lordy day, it had come to this?

"Most men would kill for what you have. You've got the world on a string."

7

"What kind of string would that be?" A string of polo ponies like the ones Mallory kept at a Kentucky horse farm? Or maybe a string of lights on a Christmas tree, when he was a guest at other people's homes?

"You're missing the point. Who knows? We may even find a wife for you." Chad's smile broadened. "Consider the trip your honeymoon."

His cousin was an expert at meddling in Mallory's life.

"That's crazy." But he might need crazy to avoid the binding clause of his father's will. The future wasn't looking good if he remained a bachelor.

"Be married by thirty–five or lose control of Thornton Enterprises. My dear Uncle Owen made that clear in his will." Chad's tone told him what he thought of the clause.

"My lawyers are working on having that nullified."

"Good luck with that. The will is ironclad."

"The board too. My word, they are on my tail like a pack of hounds. We had a rather heated discussion last week about the future direction of the company. Bunch of old codgers who should have retired long ago."

"Didn't most of them come on the board when the corporation was originally formed?"

"Exactly. My fault for not finessing some replacements. Most of them are two days older than water and may feel they are protecting my father's interests. They suggested diversification. Purely a whim. Land sakes, don't I have enough to do, flying from Bangkok to Milan for showroom openings?"

One click and Chad was back to the woman with the fierce scowl. "In a few months you'll be thirty-five."

"Time does fly when you're not having fun." Mallory rattled the ice cubes in his glass, feeling a bit pressed for time. He did hate to rush. Stripping off his pink silk tie, he stuffed it in his jacket pocket. "Not like I haven't tried. My eleven-month marriage to Rhonda was hardly a resounding success."

Chad snorted. "Good God, man. You approached your marriage like a damn business merger. Only time I saw you smile was at the bachelor party. Could be why she took up with her personal trainer."

"Hope Raoul has a wallet full of credit cards."

"Impossible to match yours." Chad's smile tweaked upward. "Credit cards, that is."

"No doubt, you rascal." Only took a few months to realize the marriage was a mistake. Mallory began to spend most of his time with his lawyers, putting together an exit package for his bride. Hardly the behavior of a newly-wed. He didn't mind Rhonda's shopping sprees, but her affair? Snatched the last sprig of spearmint from his mint julep.

He stared into his empty glass. "She seemed so right. Vice president of a bank. Attractive. Known in the area. Made perfect sense."

"Aren't we missing something? Like love?"

"Didn't she remind you of my mother?"

"Blonde. Any resemblance ends there."

Mallory's right eye started to twitch. If his mother hadn't died

three years ago, she would have seen right through Rhonda
Reynolds. "Don't know if we ever really loved each other."

"The way to a woman's heart sometimes might be our assets,
my man. A sad truth." Chad had experienced his own fair share of
disappointments.

Flat out annoyed Mallory that women might only be attracted
to his credit cards and home in Majorca, which Rhonda now
owned. He perched on the edge of the desk. "She lied to me, Chad.
Rhonda Reynolds wasn't even her real name."

"Lucy Fairchuck." Chad shook his head as he considered the
profile on the screen. "Time to put that behind us. You have to get
back in the game. And if the game helps secure your position at
Thornton Enterprises, well, saints be praised, my man. Don't know
what the board would do without you anyway, Mallory."

"Did you read the fine print in the will? Thornton Enterprises
must remain in the family. Living heirs are at a premium. My
father's side has none."

Chad slumped. "I do not need another company. I need a
happy cousin."

Following his father's sudden death, Mallory had become the
Interim CEO of Thornton Enterprises. And how he did despise
the "interim" part. The will had been a shock but not a total
surprise. Even beyond the grave, Owen Thornton held his son's
feet to the fire. Mallory had to marry and produce an heir. The rush
to comply had precipitated his disastrous marriage. His life was
turning into a mess of cold grits. A trip away sounded better by the
minute. Traveling with a stranger? Might be highly entertaining.

Drawing a deep breath, Mallory glanced back at the screen. "Why her?"

"Doesn't a woman's profession indicate her character?" Chad shot him a sly glance. "Remember math and Miss Sandusky?"

A bolt of middle school lust jolted through Mallory's body. "Miss Sandusky, as I live and breathe." When the shapely teacher wrote math problems on the board, her ponytail swayed along with her body. Every boy in the class got an immediate hard on. For Chad and Mallory, there were tutoring sessions and the scent of her Charlie perfume. Never smelled the same on girls their own age.

"She saved my sorry ass, and yours too," Chad pointed out.

"Most certainly did." Miss Sandusky believed in Mallory long after his father had thrown in the towel.

"This woman on Travel Chums is a school teacher. Says so right here."

Mallory leaned closer. "*Museum Aficionado?* What the hell is that?"

"You're no stranger to the New York Metropolitan Museum or the Louvre in Paris."

Mallory exhaled. Miriam, his executive assistant, sent both art organizations checks to make up for his absence at their fundraisers. He began to read. The twenty-seven year old English teacher lived in Chicago. Fine, upstanding Midwest stock. "Why is she looking for a man to travel with?"

Chad shrugged. "Maybe none of her friends wanted to take this particular trip, or maybe she won it as a prize. Probably the adventurous type."

"Not exactly a knockout." Was her tentative smile real, as if she wasn't quite sure about this? He knew the feeling. Straightening, he slammed his empty glass on the leather topped desk. "Consider it done. I'll behave myself. After all, I am a southern gentleman. Twin beds."

Heated towels, crisp linens, breakfast trays.

"You have to travel together." Chad's eyes issued a challenge.

Suspicion tugged at him. "Sounds like a wager. Want to sweeten the pot?" He did so enjoy a wager with his dear cousin.

Their eyes locked. Mallory sensed Chad's dilemma. What could Mallory Thornton possibly want that he didn't already have?

Chad's furrowed brow smoothed. "The custom BMW that arrived in my showroom last week."

Mallory had seen the car, all right. With subtle silver detailing, the dark gray car spoke of understated elegance. He'd considered having Chad set it aside for him. Win it? *Sweet.* The woman looked harmless enough. He'd make sure she had a good time. After Rhonda, he could go for dull as Aunt Delilah's dishwater. "Done."

His cousin swiveled back into action. "Excellent. I'll take care of filling out your profile. No photo. You don't want some shallow woman who's only interested in looks. I'll handle the details and forward any messages from her to you, or vice versa." He'd never seen Chad's fingers fly so fast.

"You know I'm Internet-challenged." Computers were a waste of time, in Mallory's book. He liked being in the thick of things, making calls, finessing deals—not hunched over a desk, pounding on a keyboard. "Miriam handles my emails."

"Only Mallory Thornton would have his executive assistant read his emails. Now, some ground rules—no using your own name or throwing gold cards around. And you have to finish up the week together."

"Fine." This was sounding more and more like some crazy romantic comedy, the kind of movie he never watched. But wasn't traveling balm for the sorry soul? Drawing in a deep breath, he nearly choked on the smell of vintage books and old money. Change of scene might revive him. A teacher should make a good tour guide.

Chad had turned, hands resting on his linen slacks. "One more thing. If you lose…"

"Never in a month of Sundays, sir."

His cousin wore the look of serious southern cogitation. "If you do not measure up…"

The glove had been thrown. "Name it."

Chad's Cheshire cat grin returned. "Just have to do it again, my man."

"Again?" The word stuck in Mallory's throat.

Looking happy as a clam at high tide, his cousin slowly nodded. "Yes, indeed. There seem to be a bevy of beauties ready to see the world."

Only took two shakes of a gator's tail. "Done, and there will be no second time."

The leather desk chair squeaked when Chad leaned back, arms behind his head. "Enjoy Italy."

"*Ciao.*" Mallory could almost feel the soft leather of the steering wheel in his hands. He'd been to Italy a few times. Might be fun to go back.

Chad fixed him with their mothers' blue eyes. "Now, understand. If you get bumped off this trip, you will have to get right back on that horse. If your sprits waver, remember your father's will."

He snorted. "Chad, I am not that desperate. I expect my legal team to come through for me with a hair-raising rebel yell."

Chad's eyebrows rose. "When the lawyers let you down, fall back on your intuition."

Mallory's stomach twisted. "Right, like that's helped me in the past."

For just a second, his cousin's cynicism slipped. "Just have a good time, buddy. Okay?"

Mallory exhaled slowly, eyes flitting back to the computer screen. "Let the games begin."

Chapter 2

Travelers shoved carry-on bags into the overhead bins and settled in for the long flight to Milan. Climbing into the middle seat of row twenty-six and plopping down, Amy smiled at the gray-haired woman next to the window. Bracketed by the arm rests, she felt hemmed in and frustrated.

Where was her travel chum? One good shove, and she jammed her green backpack under the seat in front of her. In her last e-mail, Mallory had said her flight from Savannah would land at JFK two hours ago—about an hour before Amy's own flight from Chicago. After hitting the ground, she'd stalked the waiting areas.

No slender, dark-haired woman searching for her travel chum. No Mallory.

Stomach churning, she struggled to stay calm. Digging into her backpack, Amy found the bar of Lindt dark chocolate. No rice cakes for her on this trip. Her eyes settled on the entrance to the cabin while she savored the bitter taste. This far back in economy class, she could hardly see it.

Smelling faintly of lavender, the older woman next to her turned another page of her novel. Amy swallowed the last of the chocolate square, her stomach still rebelling. If Mallory didn't show up, she'd go it alone. After all, she'd gone solo to that teachers' conference in Washington, DC, two years ago.

Both McKenna and Vanessa, high school friends, had encouraged her to call any time. They'd applauded Amy's decision to make plans with another woman on Travel Chums.

"Way to go." McKenna had chortled as they sat in Petersen's Ice Cream Parlor two days before Amy's flight. "Too bad it's not a man."

"Good grief, McKenna. I'm not you!"

Vanessa had just looked at her with soulful eyes. "Have a good time, Amy. You deserve it." She'd just come through her own trial-by-romance.

Thank goodness the wedding cancellations were all wrapped up. Felt terrible to lob the cleanup to her sister. Last time she checked in with Caitlin, her sister had sounded so preoccupied.

Grabbing her cell phone, Amy switched it to airplane mode. So darn hot in here. Reaching up, she twisted on her air jet.

The woman next to her looked up and smiled. "A bit warm, isn't it, dear?"

"A bit."

Her seatmate went back to reading. Grabbing the inflight magazine from the seat pocket, Amy flipped blindly through the pages before giving up and rolling it into a tight cylinder. Was Mallory the type who was late for everything? That would be a problem. But she'd seemed so sincere in the e-mails. Jason and Amy planned to share the costs of the wedding, including the honeymoon. When Amy asked if Mallory could forward her a small deposit requested by one of the hotels, Mallory had complied, although the check had come from a Miriam Schuster. The two must be sisters. Amy would thank Mallory from the bottom of her heart—when the woman got here.

Flight attendants closed the overhead bins with crisp efficiency. Amy tightened her seat belt and grabbed another magazine. At least she didn't have to bother with glasses anymore. Her mother and Aunt Em had given her laser surgery as a wedding gift, one present she couldn't return, although she still found herself putting on her glasses sometimes. And her hair? She patted the tortoise shell claw clip to make sure it was still in place. The blonde highlights, courtesy of Ramon, were a bit much, but McKenna had insisted on the lighter streaks as an un-wedding gift.

"Time for a lift," McKenna had chortled. "I'm having some accent streaks done myself."

Amy wasn't so sure. Her hair was now more blonde than dark honey. Shock and excitement shivered through her every time she caught sight of herself in a mirror. Who was that woman? Apparently, a woman who might be traveling alone. Amy took another bite of chocolate. She really didn't want to drive through Tuscany by herself. There was the whole issue of the stick shift.

A flurry of activity at the front door caught her attention. A tall man with a thick mane of dark hair that needed a trim had gotten on. After joking with the stewardess, he ambled down the aisle, scanning the numbers above the rows.

With a convulsive gulp, the chocolate slid down her throat.

Her sister Caitlin would call this guy a "hottie." With his broad brow, tousled hair and smoldering eyes, the newcomer was a combination of Heathcliff in *Wuthering Heights* and Edward in *Jane Eyre*. Amy had taught both novels, knowing full well that she'd never meet a man like this.

If ever there was proof of life, this man was it.

When his eyes swept her way, Amy dropped her gaze and unzipped her windbreaker. Since her concentration was zero, she jammed the magazine back into the seat pocket. Mallory might be right behind this latecomer, who held a carryon in front of him with long capable fingers. Nice hands. Jason's hands had been compact and efficient, good with a football or umpire's whistle. That was about it. He never liked to hold hands.

Amy popped the last square of chocolate into her mouth, tearing up as locker room memories raced through her mind like mental paper cuts.

But she was here to forget about Jason.

Humming under his breath, the dark-haired stranger stopped at her aisle. She heard the notes of what sounded like "Arrivederci Roma." Amy had borrowed Dean Martin's Italian CD from her mother and had been playing it since she began planning this darned honeymoon. Good grief. The newcomer's spicy scent made her think of exciting places she'd always wanted to visit. She squeezed her eyes shut, waiting for him—and her wandering thoughts—to pass.

"Miss, I just do wonder, could you by any chance be Amy?"

Her eyes flew open. "Yes." She gripped her knees with both hands. Had Mallory sent a friend, a guy-for-gods-sake, without consulting her?

"Pleased to meet you, Amy. I'm Mallory." His head dipped politely.

She shot to the edge of her seat. "But you're a man!"

Towering over her, Mallory angled his carryon into the overhead compartment. "Well, yes, I am." Only, it sounded like "Ah-am." He shrugged out of a navy sport coat and folded it, tucking it into the bin overhead.

She could barely breathe. How could this be?

The slight lift of his brows indicated that she was blowing this way out of proportion.

Hunching forward, Amy struggled out of her windbreaker. "How *could* you be a man?"

"Trust me, it comes naturally." His breath was warm on her cheek as Mallory—a male Mallory, apparently—helped her with her jacket. Bunching it up in a ball, Amy clasped it to her chest.

Sinking into the seat next to her, he snapped the seatbelt closed.

"There's been a terrible mistake." She could barely get the words out.

"Now, dearie, it will be all right." Setting her paperback aside, the woman next to the window patted Amy's hand with a knowing smile. "Men. But everything works out in the end."

Not in my world. Amy's head swiveled between the woman and Mallory. How could she continue with this trip-of-a-lifetime to the Italian Riviera, Florence and Venice…with *this* Mallory? She'd pictured chatting it up in the evening with a woman. They'd discuss art, literature and the great Italian food. Maybe they've even confide in each other about men, the rotten kind.

What had she missed in the few emails she'd sent Mallory through Travel Chums? Lord knows, she'd been a hot mess. Had she checked male instead of female when she signed up? Her mind was revving up faster than the engines.

No matter how Mallory angled his body, his legs bumped the seat in front of him. Broad shoulders expanded, and he flipped up the armrest between them. Amy shrank into herself.

An attractive stewardess edged down the aisle, checking to make sure all carry-on baggage was stowed away.

Leaning forward, Mallory directed his blue eyes to the tall brunette. "Now, when do you think that drink cart will be making the rounds? I am as thirsty as a June bug in July. Yes Ma'am, I most certainly am." His words had that soft southern drawl, apparently the kind women liked.

The attendant drew closer. "I'll see what I can do, sir." Then she nodded at Amy. "Anything for you, miss?" Her tone had leveled.

Amy massaged her forehead with one hand. "Do you have any aspirin?"

"Be right back," the attendant promised, but her eyes were on Mallory.

The thrust of the plane during takeoff pressed Amy against the back of her seat. Woozy, she clutched the armrests. When one of them moved, she realized she was gripping Mallory's forearm. He patted her hand with a warm palm, and heat surged through her.

Jerking her hands away, Amy knotted them in her lap. "Sorry."

"You're fine. Yes, you most certainly are." His low, sultry tone reverberated in her chest.

"Trust me, I'm really not."

Next to her, Mallory got comfortable, as if he had been the one to make these reservations six months ago. He rolled up the sleeves of his blue oxford cloth shirt, revealing strong forearms patterned with dark hair.

But she didn't want to think about his arms, long legs, or anything in between. She had to get her mind straight. The plane gained altitude, and an attendant took them through safety measures. What was this man thinking? Yes, she needed someone to share the expenses, but she sure hadn't been looking for a man.

Bless their hearts, Caitlin, her mother, and Aunt Em had all offered to go with her after the announcement of the canceled wedding. But one week of pity was more than Amy could bear. Besides, she hadn't told them everything. Hadn't she hurt them enough? They didn't know this mess was really her fault.

Now what was she going to do?

"Your aspirin." The perky stewardess handed a packet to Amy, along with a small bottle of water.

"Thank you." She ripped the foil open.

"Drink cart coming soon?" Mallory asked.

The stewardess beamed. "On its way."

Amy downed a mouthful of water.

"Amy, I can assure you. This is going to be a memorable trip." Mallory's smile exuded confidence.

"Did you actually think I'd be looking for a male travel chum?" Amy would appeal to his sense of reason. "I only booked one room."

Mallory's eyes widened. "Are you saying you expected a woman?"

"Of course."

Cheeks flushing, he pursed his lips. The man looked as surprised as she felt.

Amy leaned toward him until they were almost nose-to-nose. "I'm not that kind of woman, Mallory. I teach at a Catholic high school." Her voice wobbled. She pressed her lips together so tight they throbbed.

Her travel chum's blue eyes softened, like he was really trying to understand. A frown had replaced his confident smile. "Mercy, do you mean teachers don't have fun?"

"I'm not…I wouldn't…just not that kind of woman," she sputtered.

Mallory's frown deepened. Totally clueless.

The muscles in her back knotted. "That is just so, so…" Her voice shook as she searched for the word that would brand him for what he was. "Southern!"

"Sa-va-yah-nah," Mallory supplied, drawing out the name into four syllables. Then his clouded eyes brightened. With an efficient rattle, two flight attendants trundled the drink cart toward them. Mallory turned to her as if they were best of friends, or more. "Finally, refreshments. How about something to relax?"

"I *am* relaxed." The tension in her back winched tighter.

"Nonsense, why, you are just as stiff as my wrought iron fence. Let me help you with that." Mallory began to knead her shoulder gently with one hand.

Heat shimmered through her body until she could feel it in her stomach…or thereabouts.

The stewardess reached their row. "And what would you like?" she asked the woman next to the window.

"I'll have a scotch." Tucking her paperback into the seat pocket, the older woman turned. "I'm Ethel."

"Delightful. I'll have the same. Make it a double," Mallory said. "Ethel, I am Mallory. And you, Miss Amy? What would you like?"

"Amy. Just Amy. Ice water," she gasped, twisting away from Mallory and sliding lower in her seat. Maybe she needed something stronger. "Um, make that a Bloody Mary, please." Although Mallory's eyebrows rose, he said nothing.

While her seatmates sipped and chatted, Amy mentally ran through her options. She could return to the states, but the thought of giving up this trip crushed her. Or she could drive alone to Rapallo on the Italian Riviera. Financially, that would put a crimp in things. Plus, she'd be a nervous wreck. There was the whole issue of driving the rental car by herself. Jason had insisted on a stick shift. In one of her, well, *his*, e-mails, Mallory has assured her that the manual transmission was not problem.

Should have tipped her off.

Time passed slowly. Passengers settled in. She couldn't concentrate enough to read. Finally, dinner was served. At least now she had something to do. While Amy nibbled her tuna salad, Mallory and Ethel chatted about everything from football to politics. He was probably the only man she'd ever heard discuss political issues without getting into an argument. The man seemed reasonable.

Reasonable and hot.

And he sure did seem like a gentleman. But traveling together? Same bathroom, same bedroom? She wanted to be sucked right out of that plane.

From time to time, she peered over Ethel's shoulder through the small window as the plane traveled through the graying sky. Below them, white clouds mounded like thick swirls on a wedding cake. Amy's eyes filled, and she turned back to her tuna.

After the stewardess made a final sweep through the cabin, Mallory settled back. His cologne reminded her of the woods at dusk—definitely not the soapy smell of Jason emerging from the locker room.

That locker room.

Reaching up, Amy turned her air jet on full blast. She was taking this trip, no matter what.

Eventually, the cabin darkened and the movie began. Slipping on her headset, Amy did some deep breathing. How hard could it be to drive a stick shift? She'd tackle that challenge first before the issue of sharing a bathroom. Her stomach fluttered as she sneaked peeks at Mallory—his clothes, the way he handled himself. Didn't she tell her students that characters were revealed through actions and dialogue?

Did rapists and murderers wear tasseled loafers and talk about football players and their abuse of power? She didn't think so.

Tension drained from her body, like someone had pulled the

plug in the bath tub. For just one week, she'd become the type of woman who *would* travel with a handsome stranger. For just one week, why not "let loose," as Caitlin put it? Amy's shoulders squeezed together in excitement. How totally not her.

Anxiety followed close on the heels of that dizzying thrill. How did a girl who'd gone to Immaculate Heart of Mary High School, where she now taught, go about letting loose?

Chapter 3

He was going to kill Chad.

Knees embedded in the seat in front of him, Mallory silently cursed the cramped quarters of economy class—and his cousin.

Seemed that Chad had purposely stacked the deck against him. Again.

In the darkened cabin, Mallory's mind rearranged the pieces on his chess board. Arriving late had obviously been a good idea. He'd hidden out in the First Class Priority Lounge for the two hours between flights. Took a shower, watched some golf on TV. Not a good idea to give Amy any time to decide he wasn't her type.

Her type? He hadn't expected his gender to be a surprise. The high school teacher was as alarmed as Scarlett when she heard Atlanta was burning. He'd deal with his cousin later. Right now, he had to ease Amy into her comfort zone. Reassure her that he would, of course, be a gentleman.

His right eye began to twitch.

A little uptight, but Amy Shaw had a certain appeal. How often did he come across a woman not starved almost beyond recognition? By the time of their divorce, Rhonda's cheeks were sunken and her hips jutted from her Dolce and Gabbana slacks like shale ledges.

Amy's generous curves bloomed in a ripe and appealing fashion. The glasses from her photo were gone, and her green eyes sparkled when she got upset—which seemed to be often. And her hair? Well, it most certainly was not brown. Tied back, her honey-colored hair was shot through with blonde, but not the metallic platinum that had been Rhonda's choice.

Was Amy Shaw attractive? Yes. Was she a prickly pear? Most definitely.

Chad had set the bar high. Mallory didn't know quite how to play this, but he sure didn't want to be crossing this ocean again the following day if his travel chum decided to continue on alone. How could he convince Amy he was prepared to treat her like a sister? That would probably be the best tactic. Give the poor woman a berth as wide as the marshes that cushioned Savannah from coastal storms. Could separate rooms be in the budget, whatever that might be?

Life as Mallory Schuster was supposed to be frugal. His thoughts circled that word with cautious respect. At Chad's insistence, he'd borrowed the last name of his assistant, Miriam Schuster. Chad had even come up with a story about the two siblings, Miriam and Mallory, sharing a check book. Without a question, Miriam had sent Amy the requested deposit check. Miriam had worked for his father for years and was well versed in the art of discretion.

Mallory shifted in his seat. This wager had felt like a lark when he'd been playing a game over the Internet through his cousin Chad. For a few days, excitement had coursed through his veins at the thought of a teacher who wanted to travel with a stranger.

Granted, some form of Miss Sandusky had fevered his brain.

Now he felt like an idiot. He'd been skunked.

When Amy's eyes brimmed with tears, he was at a loss. Mallory Thornton—at a loss.

Until she laughed.

Amy's laugh told a whole different story than that tight topknot. In the darkened cabin, they watched the movie *Airport*, a classic comedy. Her girlish giggle lightened the close cabin air, and her lightly freckled nose crinkled in the cutest way. Even with his headsets on, he could hear that laugh, and he chuckled in response.

At the end of the movie, the lights in the cabin dimmed. After pulling a pair of eyeshades from the seat pocket in front of her, Amy adjusted them and hunkered down, stuffing a flat pillow behind her head. Almost as an afterthought, she yanked the elastic from her hair. Land sakes, long curls spilled over her shoulders, pale sherry glowing under shimmering blonde streaks.

Damn. Soft curls had always been one of Mallory's weaknesses. Shortly after the wedding, Rhonda had cut her hair into a short cap with sharp angles. Unbecoming as hell, not that he'd said anything.

Amy's curls smelled enticing—like oranges sitting in the sun on his side porch while Nellie, his doting housekeeper, served breakfast. With a slight shake of her shoulders, the testy teacher had become a different woman.

Sexy but subtle. His muscles tightened.

Amy's figure did credit to the dark green T-shirt with *Read It!* scrawled in white across the chest. And yet, her shoulders and arms

28

looked so delicate, almost fragile as she turned slightly toward him, trying to find a comfortable spot. Mallory busied himself with his blanket to hide his own confusion.

"Warm enough?" he murmured, bending closer to the curls. "Would a blanket help?"

"Yes, please." She sighed.

Lifting the navy rectangle airlines called a blanket, Mallory draped it over her body, watching it cup her curves. A drowsy smile tilted the corners of her lips.

A sleeping woman could be as sexy as hell.

When an attendant moved down the aisle with more plastic packages, Mallory motioned for one. Fortunately he had no trouble sleeping on planes or anywhere else, even in close quarters. Ripping open the packet, he shook the blanket over himself. Damn things were like handkerchiefs.

The only sounds were the drone of the plane and Ethel's light snoring.

Then Amy sighed again. The eyeshade slipped, and her eyes blinked open. Clearly she was troubled. Mallory's guilt came washing back, like bad pulled pork.

Time to smooth the waters. Leaning toward her, he inhaled the tangy scent of those curls. Long tawny lashes feathered onto her cheeks. "Amy, Ah am so sorry if this isn't exactly what you'd planned."

"Not what I'd planned!" Her head shot straight up. Right into his nose.

"For God's sake, woman!" He reared back in agony. Bright red drops of blood splattered onto his slacks.

"Oh! I'm sorry, so sorry!" Stooping, Amy dug around in her backpack. "What have I done?"

Signaling for the stewardess, Mallory grabbed a handkerchief from his back pocket. His nose hurt like hell when he pressed the white linen against his nostrils. "Ma'am, I wonder if I might have some ice?" he asked the flight attendant.

"Of course, sir. Right away."

"Is the bleeding bad?" Amy clutched a fistful of tissues.

Lifting the handkerchief, Mallory wrinkled his nose. Another sizeable drop of red hit the front of his khaki pants.

Amy shook her head in disapproval. "No, you have to pinch it at the top."

He gripped the tip of his nose with two fingers.

"Wrong end, wrong end. Here let me." Brushing his fingers and the bloodied handkerchief aside, she gripped the top ridge of his nose with almost clinical efficiency.

Land sakes, he certainly would not want her handling any other stiff part of his body.

"Better?" she asked.

Mallory was beginning to think this applying pressure thing had its advantages. Amy's curls tickled his cheek, soft and scented. As her breathing quickened, her breasts rose and fell with a hypnotic rhythm.

"Does this feel better?" Amy peered down at him.

"Much better."

Taking her hand away slowly, she wrenched the blanket back up around her shoulders. "I just don't see how this happened."

Mallory settled back. "I believe you smashed into my face."

"That's not what I meant." Amy nibbled on her bottom lip, brows pinched together. "I just had to find someone to travel with me after…"

"After what?" Good lord, he wanted to hug her.

What was there about a woman in distress? Chad always said that was his problem. When he'd met Rhonda, she gave him some cock and bull story about a terminally ill mother. Yet somehow, her mother had managed a spirited, although drunken, salsa at their wedding reception.

"The mix-up is upsetting," he said, shifting in his seat and relishing the thoughts of just how he might make Chad pay for this juvenile prank. Drawing and quartering would be too kind. "I've, ah, saved for this trip…for a long time." Right, would his nose start to grow like Pinocchio's? He could have paid for fifty of these trips and not even made a dent in his holdings. Rhonda had only gone for trips with beaches. Museums definitely were not her thing.

Amy blinked. "What happened? You didn't plan on traveling alone either?"

"My life took a different turn."

"Oh, gosh." Such sadness in her face.

He leaned closer. "You know, Amy, if both of us really want this trip and the, well, sights…" Where were they going after they landed in Milan? For the life of him, he could not remember. He'd been so caught up in the Franklin acquisition that he'd left everything to Chad. The forwarded emails blurred in his mind.

Museums and galleries. He thought it had to do with those.

Amy's long lashes were darkened by tears. Where was he? *Focus.*
Treat this like a merger or an acquisition.

"Of course, I respect your concern, when for some reason you
thought I was a woman, but couldn't we share a room? Separate
beds of course. A compromise might work for both of us."

Negotiation. Always a good chip to play in any board room.

Amy went back to gnawing her full lower lip. "Oh, I don't
know, Mallory."

Time to regain ground. "I'd certainly respect your privacy, and I
know you'd respect mine." The last part was an afterthought, but
he could see it had an effect.

"You're right, I guess." Amy seemed to be analyzing every
word. "I don't want to give up this trip, and I certainly don't want
to ruin it for you."

Reveille was sounding. "Perhaps we could take two rooms? An
expense, but I would be happy to make up any difference." Hell's
bells. Chad wasn't here and he'd never know.

"We'll work it out." She set her chin. That delicate point
prodded his heart.

Nose throbbing, he settled back. Forget the car and the
company, for now. He was more concerned about keeping that
sweet smile on her face.

Let loose. Relieved to be on the ground, Amy picked up the pace as
they trekked toward the car rental counter. With a new, sexy
swagger, she tried to channel Caitlin.

Mid-stride, her eyes slid sideways. Mallory Schuster, a.k.a. Heathcliff, was incredibly handsome. Plus, he seemed to be a decent sort of guy. After all, wasn't he interested in art museums? Excitement bubbled through her like a freshly opened bottle of pop. If she pushed up her sleeves, she'd see goose bumps.

Come hell or high water, she was going to let loose. All week.

One week with him in the same bedroom? She stumbled. Mallory half turned, one hand outstretched. Gripping the handle of her suitcase more tightly, she waved him on. "I'm fine."

The dark stubble on Mallory chin and cheeks gave him a cosmopolitan look, like he should be on some HBO show. "Lives of the Rich and Famous." No doubt he dated sophisticated women who wore a size two, dressed in designer clothes, and traveled to Europe every year. These women may have seen the movie *Wuthering Heights*, but they'd never actually read the book. That may be more Mallory Schuster's type. The excitement in her stomach twisted into anxiety.

No lesson plan could have prepared her for this. She'd have to wing it. The thought sent her tight stomach tumbling, as if she'd just dropped out of the sky. How relieved she was to finally see the car rental counter ahead. Now if she could just manage the darn stick shift.

While Amy talked to the clerk, Mallory stepped back. He always wound up squiring women who depended on him for the plans. Now he regarded the lush blonde in the safari pants and T-shirt with respect. He'd nearly landed on his ass watching her backside as she trotted through the baggage area. She didn't flaunt her figure, didn't even seem aware of her curves. Just moved with confidence.

Confidence was sexy.

Chad had chosen well. Mallory's usual tactics with women might not cut it. Amy Shaw may be a woman who did not need or want a man—at least not long term. This was like fanning open a poker hand and not knowing which card to play. Didn't happen often.

"Here we go, Mallory. Up ahead. Slot fifty-five." Keys in hand, Amy pointed toward the numbered row of parked cars.

He swallowed hard. In rental space fifty-five sat a practical blue hatchback. He could picture a pack of howling teenage girls crammed into it on their way to some sporting event. With longing, Mallory's mind caressed his sweet black Jag or reveled in the rumble of his vintage Corvette. He could hardly believe he was about to spend one week driving this nondescript rental.

Or maybe not. While he hoisted luggage into the hatchback, Amy had gotten behind the wheel. By the time he crammed himself into the passenger seat, her head was bent over a large map.

She glanced up. "How about being navigator?"

"I'd be happy to drive," he offered, pushing his seat back.

"I can handle it if you'll check the directions."

"Sure." Mallory took the map from her trembling hands. "You okay?"

"I'm fine." When she gripped the steering wheel with both

hands, the trembling stopped. Body rigid, Amy studied the console. Reaching into one of the many pockets in her pants, she pulled out one of those rubber things and swept her hair back. Not an improvement, in his book. Then she jammed the key into the ignition, turned it, and ground the gearshift into reverse.

Mallory clamped his jaw shut. He would not say a word, not even if it killed him. And it might.

The car lurched as Amy backed out of the slot. Dropping the map, he braced himself with one hand on the dash and the other on the door handle.

Amy continued to wrestle with the gearshift. "Looks like we pick up A7 and then head straight for the coast. Southwest," she gritted out.

A woman who understood directions. Mallory's confidence in her grew. As she hit the clutch again, she glanced pointedly at the map that had fallen to the floor.

"Right." Loosening his grip on the dash, Mallory scooped up the map and snapped it open with both hands, just to keep them steady.

How could he persuade her to let him drive?

"The route should be very picturesque," Amy muttered between clenched teeth while the gears continued to grind. The car was quivering in protest, like a race horse under the whip. Somehow they made it out of the terminal and onto a highway. He visited his showroom in Milan quite often. They seemed to be on the right track.

Glancing out the window, Mallory wondered if he would end

up dead in one of the ditches. His neck began to ache, and he wondered if it was whiplash. "So, do you drive a stick shift often in Indiana?"

"Illinois," she corrected him. "Oak Park. West suburb of Chicago. My, ah, friend wanted the stick."

"The one who couldn't make it at the last minute?" Amy had mentioned that in one of the emails Chad had forwarded to him. She had planned on traveling with a friend, but something happened.

Amy licked her lips. "Right."

The traffic picked up speed. The gears ground one more time, and the car rocketed forward.

"Good God." She was going to kill him.

"Are you all right?" When Amy leaned toward him, the car followed her, veering to the right.

Mallory grabbed the wheel. "Please pull over." He angled the steering wheel to take them onto the shoulder.

Color flamed high in her cheeks, but she brought the car to the side of the road and stopped. Grit blew along the highway as he pushed the door open and dug himself from the front seat. Circling the front of the car, Mallory considered how to handle this. At this point, she could still send him right back to Milan and the states.

That was sure as hell not going to happen.

Chapter 4

Springing from the car, Amy faced him, arms crossed and right hand clutching the key. "What? So it takes me a while."

"Please, let me help out. A stick shift isn't easy if you're not used to it. Glad to drive. After all, we're partners."

Amy's tears brimmed like a line of diamonds under each eye. Was she that sensitive?

Lips trembling, she dropped the keys into his hands. "Fine. Your turn."

Saints be praised. While she circled around to the passenger side, Mallory slid behind the wheel. Adjusting the seat, he started the car and scooped the map off the floor. "Sure could use a navigator."

When Amy smiled, her eyes were the color of a putting green, warm and full of hope. "No problem." She took the map in her long elegant fingers. Settling into the seat, he pulled back into the traffic. After a few miles, Amy seemed to relax. The overnight flight was never easy. He snapped on the radio, and the unmistakable beat of the Big Bopper singing "Blueberry Hill" filled the car. He just about split a gut laughing, and Amy was right there with him.

"No fair." She gave the dashboard a playful pat. "I want romantic Italian music."

"*Romantic* Italian music?"

"Is there any other kind?" With a little shake of her head, she looked away and cracked open her window.

Time to keep his eyes on the road. The sleeves of Amy's jacket were pushed up, and sunlight played along the down on her arms. Smelling of the countryside, the breeze teased her hair from that damn rubber band thing. Curls danced around her face. She kept brushing them out of her eyes, but she didn't close the window.

Inhaling became a pleasure. The sun bounced off the hood, and Mallory adjusted his sunglasses. At least he wasn't in the air-conditioned seclusion of his office, taking calls and strategizing with his global managers. Miriam had texted him a couple of times about the Franklin deal, and he'd answered her questions while he waited for Amy at the rental counter. For now, he'd turned his phone off.

"Had you planned this trip for a long time?" he asked. How on earth had she ended up traveling alone?

After digging around in her backpack, Amy snapped on a pair of sunglasses. "About six months. Maybe we should concentrate on the road."

"Said like a school teacher."

Amy stiffened.

"Sorry." He suppressed a smile. "It's just that sometimes…"

"I know, I know. I sound like a school teacher because I *am* a school teacher. People tell me that all the time. So shoot me." She looked insulted.

Took Mallory a second to gather his thoughts. "Salt of the

earth. I have a great deal of respect for teachers." Thinking back to Miss Sandusky, he mentally added "lust" to that respect.

"Good. I'm glad." The look she gave him brimmed with so much trust that guilt came creeping back. He liked to earn people's trust.

Blowing out a sigh, he sank deeper into his seat. Might as well enjoy the ride. Vineyards on rolling hillsides. Fields of sunflowers. He was in Italy—the country of great food, friendly people, and fields that sure didn't smell like the city. This crazy bet had brought him here. Time to enjoy it.

He could kill Chad later.

Before long, they pulled into a rest stop. Beyond the gas pumps stretched a long, low deli. He parked the car to the side and got out. Amy stretched like a kitten in the sunlight, but he wasn't going there.

"Hungry?" she asked.

"Starved." Opening the door of the deli, he was met with the pungent aroma of sausages and cheeses, with an underpinning of basil. Not like the typical gas stop in the states. His stomach rumbled.

After surveying the display case, Amy ducked to the side and asked the woman behind the register a question. "Be right back," she told him. "Restrooms are next door."

"Seasonings?" the man behind the counter asked.

"Well now, I'll just enjoy what you give me." His eyes were on Amy. As she walked out, she flung her head back and pulled out that rubber thingie. Her hair sparkled in the sunlight like a good chardonnay. His head reeled from the sudden vision of that fragrant abundance flung across a pillow.

Land of mercy. Rein it in, Mallory. After all, there was something innocent about Amy Shaw. The wager felt so wrong. He didn't like that feeling one bit.

Huddled at the entrance to the ladies' room, Amy dug her phone from her backpack. She was a woman in bad need of advice. "Caitlin, pick up. Please pick up."

Her sister answered on the second ring.

"Help," Amy squeaked in a small voice.

"Amy, are you all right? What's Allie like?"

"Mallory," Amy corrected her. "And *he's* not a woman."

"What?"

"Mallory is a man." Amy's dry lips caught on each *m*. "We're on the road to Rapallo, and I'm, well, trying not to panic."

"Attractive? Interesting?"

"Yes, and does that matter?"

Her sister groaned. "Um, yeah, it helps! I mean, he's not some psycho, right?"

"So far, no."

"Take a deep breath. Is he hitting on you?"

"No. Should he be?" As far as Amy knew, Mallory had not even made one pass. The backpack slid from her arm.

"Maybe he just wants a companion who enjoys the same stuff. Didn't you tell me you listed yourself as 'Museum Aficionado'? He's probably into the art scene, like you." All kinds of noise blared in the background. Amy could hardly hear her sister.

"Where are you? You must have the TV on awfully loud in the shirt shop."

"Here's the thing, Amy," Caitlin began, a note of hesitation in her voice. "When it looked like the wedding was off…"

Her thudding heart broke into a gallop.

"When it looked like you might have to go to Italy alone…or with a stranger…we decided—Kurt and I—that maybe we should surprise you."

Kurt had been Caitlin's live-in boyfriend for about two years. Men hovered around Caitlin like fruit flies on a humid summer day.

"Surprise me how?"

"We're here!" Caitlin sounded jubilant.

"Where?" Her hand had gone numb.

"In Rapallo! Kurt said we should have done this sooner."

"You mean *you're* on *my* honeymoon?" Amy slumped against the white cinder block wall.

"Right, I wanted to show some support, Amy, and surprise you. Then you got this travel chum. Never thought you'd actually carry through on that. Who knew? Great day for the beach." Amy could hear Caitlin yawn. "We're going back to the room to shower. Hey, where are you?"

Dazed, Amy stared out at the highway. "I have no idea."

"That's not like you."

"Do you mean you just picked up and left work?" Amy was still trying to wrap her mind around Caitlin's news.

"Isn't that great? Laura said she could handle the shop. Kurt had just finished a corporate website project. The other two guys were totally comfortable handling his office, so we were good." Kurt and some of his college friends had built a successful website company after graduation. They had a small office in Oak Park near Caitlin's shirt shop.

"Only you could make this work," Amy groaned.

Years ago, if school was canceled because of snow, Caitlin was the first one into her snowsuit and out the door to make an igloo. Amy would open her books at the kitchen table so she could keep up with her school work.

"See you soon, Amy, okay?" Caitlin sang in a chipper voice, almost like an invitation, almost like she'd been the one to organize this trip.

"Right. Soon." Amy ended the call. When had everything gotten so out of control? She felt as if she'd bought a ticket for the merry-go-round at the state fair and instead had ended up on Son of Beast. How could she let loose with Caitlin around? Her sister already had that niche filled.

Gathering her courage, she fluffed one hand through her newly tinted tresses. She'd never been a quitter.

When she returned to the car, Mallory had slid back into the driver's seat. Thank goodness. That stick shift was a nightmare.

One arm cocked out the open window and the breeze ruffling his hair, he was giving full attention to his sandwich. Those aviator sunglasses added to his mystery, and butterflies jittered in her stomach.

Who was Mallory Schuster anyway? He sure wasn't a teacher.

The girls at Immaculate Heart of Mary High School would go crazy if this man ever walked down the halls. With his dark good looks, Mallory might even be more attractive than Rich Daley, their beach boy biology teacher.

Snapping the seat belt closed, she turned to her travel chum. "Ready?"

"You bet. Hope this is all right. I figured I couldn't go wrong with anything they had." Mallory handed her the bag.

"Smells wonderful." Amy unwrapped the baguette, dripping in olive oil. Sinking her teeth into the fresh crust, she took a healthy bite. The cheeses were soft and delicately flavored, overlaid with sun-dried tomatoes and fresh basil. She licked the oil at the corners of her mouth. "Delicious."

This wasn't the time to be thinking about the room. The room that may have one bed or two. The room with one bathroom they had to share.

Chapter 5

Five minutes later, they were headed toward the coast. The dampness from the sea wafted through the open windows, bathing her face. After the dry air of the plane, the moist air felt wonderful. Although she couldn't see any water yet, Amy pictured gulls, stretches of sandy beach, and wet towels drying in the sun. A pretty heady mixture combined with the deep, woodsy scent rolling off Mallory Schuster. He hummed as he took the turns.

Jason would never have been comfortable on the twisting roads of the Italian coastline. Oh, he'd never admit it, but her former fiancé would probably be tapping the brakes. Mallory, on the other hand, was a whole different story. With the glee of a teenager, he handled the steering wheel with his left hand while he worked the gearshift with the other. Sure, sometimes his lips would purse with irritation when the gears screamed. But he always got the car to settle down. Totally amazing. She'd bet one month's pay that this wasn't the kind of car he drove back in Savannah.

They rounded a bend in the narrow road.

"Oh, my!" Amy's breath left her body with a whoosh. As far as the eye could see, the sea stretched below them—a broad expanse of rippling aqua water that turned darker blue while white clouds drifted lazily overhead.

Mallory threw her a boyish grin. "Puts Florida to shame, doesn't it?"

Suspicion pierced her contentment. "I thought you'd never been here."

For a moment, Mallory hesitated, lips moving, as if searching for the right word. "I've seen pictures. My word, this traffic is really picking up." Mouth set, he trained his eyes over the wheel.

Amy squinched down in the bucket seat. Since she was already feeling uncomfortable, maybe this was the time to broach the subject of her sister. "One thing I wanted to mention, my sister might also be in Rapallo with her boyfriend."

Mallory's right eyebrow quirked upward. "Might?"

Amy began to fan herself with the map. "Right. Caitlin thought it might be fun…to join the party."

She certainly wasn't going to tell him her sister was rescuing her from a solitary honeymoon. No way was she going to bring up her broken engagement. Her mother had been so disappointed about the canceled wedding. Not only had Amy lost a fiancé and a bucket load of deposits, she'd also postponed the arrival of grandchildren, one of her mother's lifetime goals.

One of Amy's goals too. She'd always wanted a big family, scads of kids running around the house. "My family's a bit unpredictable," she told Mallory, clutching the door handle as he accelerated into another turn.

The fact that Caitlin and Kurt would go to this trouble and take on the expense troubled her a bit. Their concern was so darn sweet. Apparently, Caitlin hadn't believed Amy's Travel Chum story and wanted to make sure her sister didn't take this trip alone. How great was that?

"My word, your sister must be very spontaneous." Admiration rang in Mallory's voice.

"Do you have siblings?"

He shook his head. "Only child. You get all the attention and all the blame. But I do have a cousin."

"Cousins count."

His chuckle qualified as a locker room guffaw. "Chad's a good man. Crazy, but a good man."

"Family is always good."

"Sometimes."

Opening the window wider, she let the breeze wash over her. Her shoulders loosened. Nothing would spoil these few days as an experienced woman of the world. She was going to work every tool in her toolbox.

Her right hand tightened on the door handle.

Just what did a worldly woman have in her toolbox?

When they reached Rapallo, the traffic got crazy. Mallory shifted down, edging the car down narrow roads that made Savannah's cobblestone streets seem spacious. This place had "vacation" written all over it, from the sunburned tourists in bathing suits to the piles of suitcases in front of the hotels.

"So, many museums here?" he asked as they crawled along. How did a beach town like Rapallo fit in the plans of a woman crazy about art museums?

His travel chum frowned. "No, why?"

"Wasn't that what this trip was about?"

Amy blinked, a fox sensing the hounds are near. "We…I, er, thought it would be…a nice place to start."

Start what? Mallory didn't even want to ask. He'd had enough sharing for one day. Jet lag was starting to set in.

With a sudden jerk, Amy craned her long neck toward the windshield. "There it is! Hotel Giulio Cesare." She checked the map.

As he drove closer, Mallory considered the pink stucco structure with approval. Not bad. The quintessential beach hotel might have been found in Palm Springs in the 1920s. Charming but not grand. Close to the beach.

His shirt was sticking to his back. How long had it been since his shower before the flight? What he wouldn't give for the spacious shower in his Savannah mansion, the powerful jets set at every angle for a hot water massage.

Traveling always carried trade-offs. For now, he was here. And he was glad.

Cars inched through the streets, people hanging from the windows, voices high as they called to each other with broad gestures. Music blaring from car radios. Palm trees everywhere with the sound of water in the background. Bougainvillea clinging to the walls of hotels and shops in thick waves of fuchsia. Bright pink petunias and trailing ivy spilling from balconies and window boxes.

Color. Atmosphere. Change of scenery.

Rapallo was not Savannah.

The weight of Thornton Enterprises, his father's directive, and his failed marriage lifted. Mallory hadn't felt this carefree in a long time.

When they pulled up in front of the hotel, not a porter was in sight. Must be a busy place. He parked. After helping Amy out of the car—not that she was one to wait for him to open the door— he began pulling out the luggage. "I could use a shower."

"Shower?" Amy froze, eyes wide as the sunflowers they'd passed on the road.

He set her suitcase down. "Why don't you go first?"

"Thank you." Yanking her T-shirt over the waistband of her cargo pants, Amy straightened her shoulders. The heat had molded the green shirt to her body. He forced himself to look away and reached for his navy bag. This chum thing might prove more difficult than he'd planned.

Ahead of him, Amy marched through the doorway, tugging her bag behind her. He grabbed the handle of his suitcase and followed her inside. Although a welcome relief, the air conditioning pasted the grit to his skin.

Inside, the reception area of the hotel was done in yellow tile with a blue accent. Bright. Cheerful. Small palm trees and ferns gave it an exotic look. Behind the registration desk, a short, round man yelled into an old-fashioned phone in Italian. Finally, he ended the conversation, slammed down the receiver and planted both hands flat on the counter. "*Buon giorno.* What can I do today for you, ah, today?"

"We have a reservation." Amy stepped up to the counter.

"Under the name of Shaw."

The man ran one finger down the lines of a huge ledger open on the desk. "Ah, yes, yes. Here. *Sì, sì.* Signora Shaw."

Amy unfolded the confirmation and pushed the paper toward him. "But now we would really like two rooms, not one."

The man shook his head. "No is possible, signora. Full. *Capishe?*" He flung out his arms as if to encompass the entire establishment.

"We'll take what you have." Edging around Amy, Mallory tried to slide his gold card onto the counter. After all, hadn't Chad invalidated their terms of engagement by not telling Amy he was a man?

Amy's hand stopped him. Eyes blazing, she produced her own credit card. He drew back while she completed the transaction.

Land sakes, had the lines been drawn?

The concierge nodded. "One room, two beds. You will find elevator in back." He handed Amy the keycard.

Together they walked toward the antique brass door of the elevator and waited. Finally, the doors swung open with a ping, and a couple stepped out. A pretty blonde cuddled against her companion. He loved to see couples that into each other.

"Caitlin?" Amy stepped forward. "Kurt?"

"Amy!" The blonde flung her arms wide.

Amazing. Must be the sister. Something in his chest pinched. Scenes like this reminded him that he was an only child.

"So you're *here.*" Amy pointed to the tiled floor.

"Right, we got the last room. Isn't that fabulous?" Caitlin's eyes were on Mallory.

"Y'all came to join the party?" He stepped forward. "I'm Mallory. Mallory...Schuster."

As they shook hands, Caitlin's eyes danced. "So glad to meet you. A little surprising but nice."

"Your sister was surprised too." Horrified might be more like it.

"Oh, I'll just bet she was."

Amy's face brightened. "Wait. Okay. You have a room here, right?" She looked from Mallory to Kurt. "So the guys could bunk together, and you and I could share a room."

Kurt's face went blank.

Caitlin frowned. "No chance, Amy."

"But it's perfect. A solution." Amy's voice rose with hope.

The couple began edging toward the front door. Mallory stifled a laugh.

"We don't need a solution, Amy." Caitlin took her boyfriend's hand. "We're, ah, already solved."

Pausing when they reached the hotel entrance, Amy's sister and her boyfriend were outlined by the bright sunlight. High time to enjoy that beach.

"You two have fun," Caitlin threw back. "I mean, get settled. Wait'll you see the beach."

Shoulders slumping, Amy looked so forlorn. "See you later."

Kurt waved and then tugged Caitlin into the sunlight.

Mallory definitely had to get Amy into her comfort zone. "Come on. Let's check out the room. See if you like it. We can leave the luggage here while you decide." He pushed their bags against the wall under one of the gilded mirrors.

Amy stepped into the small elevator. "What if we don't like the room?"

He pushed the button for the third floor. "We always have options." Like what? He had no desire to begin looking for another hotel at this late date.

Checking out the room was all about giving her choices. Putting her in control. Staring at the blinking buttons as the elevator climbed, Mallory knew they'd both lost any sense of where they were going.

Chapter 6

Caitlin was here, in the same hotel? Amy's amazement quickly simmered into frustration. How could Amy reinvent herself with her younger sister on the scene? Amy would always be "Big Dumpling" as long as "Little Dumpling" was around. Her father had lovingly nicknamed his daughters after Caitlin was born. Amy wished she'd had a vote.

Hands shaking, she jammed the keycard into the lock of the room she would share for two nights with Mallory Schuster. It clicked open. Reaching over her shoulder with one muscled arm, Mallory shoved the door wide. His musky male scent rolled over her.

"More like a closet than a room." His voice dropped a notch.

"Lovely." Shaking out her legs, she stepped inside. A nightstand was wedged between two twin beds. Thank goodness the staff had received her email changing the queen-size bed to two twins. At the time, Amy thought a woman would be sleeping in the other bed.

"At least three feet between the beds. Plenty of room." Mallory cupped one hand over his chin. Was he hiding a smile?

"Did I say I was measuring?"

"Is the bathroom this small?"

"Check it out for yourself." Amy was already sweeping back the long billowing sheers. When she pulled the French doors open, a warm, humid breeze rushed in. Licking her lips, she tasted the sea.

A sense of well-being filled her as she stepped onto the small balcony. Italy. Husband or no husband, she'd made it here alone. Well, except for Mallory. And Caitlin. Extending her hands along the wrought iron railing, she smiled.

Mallory had picked up the phone, but after a few seconds, he put it down and came up behind her. Putting out one hand, he tested the railing. "Careful now. Might not be sturdy enough to lean on." His eyes were the color of the water folding onto the shore below in soft waves.

"Oh, I'll be careful."

Lines crinkled from his eyes when his gaze met hers. "Sometimes you can be too careful."

"Really? Don't know if I've ever had that happen." Giddiness spiraled through her chest and pooled between her legs, leaving her light-headed. Stepping back into the room, she relished the solid tile floor beneath her feet.

Mallory edged toward the door. "The desk isn't answering. Think I'll run back down for the luggage."

"Thank you," Amy murmured, turning back to study the room as the door closed behind him. Hearing his footstep recede down the hallway, she grabbed her phone. "McKenna, pick up, pick up." Should be late evening in Chicago, but her midwife friend could be delivering a baby.

"Hey, what's up, Amy? Did you land safely?"

"Safely? I don't know. Caitlin's here, McKenna. She surprised me and came for moral support. Had already made the plans when I posted on Travel Chums."

"Excellent! Three women enjoying the trip together. Wouldn't be my choice, but it sounds like…fun."

"Not really. My travel chum turned out to be a man, and Caitlin brought her boyfriend."

Her friend's hoot could probably be heard out in the hallway. Amy stepped closer to the window.

"So your Mallory's a man?" Delight lifted her friend's voice." "I love it! What's he like?"

"He's not *my* Mallory, and he's hot. Gorgeous doesn't begin to cover it. Southern."

"That's awesome! See? Lose a bonehead, gain a hottie. Karmic law."

Maybe she should have called Vanessa instead of McKenna. A mother, Vanessa might be have been more grounded.

"Amy, are you there?"

"Barely. Okay, McKenna, here's where I am. I decided to go for it. I mean, make the most of it. But Caitlin's arrival really threw me. You know I was always Big Dumpling compared to her."

"That nickname was your father's bad joke. Forget it. Besides, sometimes I think your sister could be anorexic. Get over it. You're in Italy! Caitlin's there so you're good. You don't know this Mallory person, and it's good to have a sister around while you check him out. Southern, huh? Justin Timberlake is from the South. They make hotties there."

"Very southern. Savannah."

"Three words, Amy. Be a babe." McKenna's reckless chortle attacked the knot in Amy's neck. "What are you wearing?"

"My cargo pants and a T-shirt."

"Remember that bag I told you to pack?"

"Right. I barely fit it in my luggage. Didn't peek, just as you said." You didn't cross McKenna.

"Time to break it open. Enjoy!"

"Okay, but got to go. He could come back any minute."

"You can only hope." McKenna was still laughing when they hung up.

Pressing the phone to her lips, Amy scrutinized the room.

These beds weren't far enough apart.

With a few creaks and groans, the elevator slowly descended.

Good God, Amy had just about taken out a measuring tape to gauge the distance between the two beds. He'd put a quick call in to Miriam to change the reservations in Florence. Chad didn't ever have to know. When traveling, Mallory liked soft carpet, dim lights, warm towels. Miriam would see to it. Somehow Mallory would make all this acceptable to Amy.

When the elevator doors swept open, he stepped out and grabbed the handles of the two suitcases. Seconds later, he was punching the button for the third floor.

His thoughts raced as the elevator climbed. Could Amy Shaw really be this sweet? Probably not. Most women were devious. Hadn't he learned that with Rhonda? From her name to her family background, she'd had a mind as creative as General Oglethorpe when he designed Savannah. But Rhonda proved sadly lacking in the general's ethics.

Well, this was a wager, not a wedding. Short week.

The elevator bounced to a halt on the third floor, and Mallory tugged the bags through the narrow hallway, trying hard not to scrape the walls. His mother had been very patient with the servants, but marring the walls meant no hush puppies for one week. Mallory did so love the deep fried bits of cornmeal.

After he hustled their bags into the room, Amy and Mallory stepped around each other carefully as they unpacked. This was like shooting hoops with the guys and trying not to foul. The room was even smaller than his dressing room at home.

"Would you like to shower?" He thought he'd come back and find her in the bathroom. Wasn't that what women did…take total control as if they were Sherman, marching through Georgia?

"No, you go first. I just didn't want to leave all this yet." Amy got this dreamy look on her face and turned back to the balcony.

Certainly not going to argue. Grabbing some fresh clothes, he sandwiched himself into the bathroom. Lordy. Felt like he'd walked directly into a closet…with running water. But once inside the tiny shower, those picayune points dissolved in the blistering hot water. After a few minutes, he switched to ice cold. Time to douse the totally inappropriate thoughts about his travel chum.

How had Amy become confused with Miss Sandusky in his mind?

When he emerged from the bathroom ten minutes later, Amy

was folding what looked like personal items into a drawer. Wedged between the open french door and the bathroom, they faced each other. Her neck and cheeks reddened as she slammed the drawer shut and brushed that flowing hair back from her face. Were her cheeks silky soft like the curls that had tumbled over him on the plane? Almost worth getting his nose cracked.

Amy's eyes focused on his chin.

"What?" He ran one hand over his face.

"You must have been in a hurry," she murmured in a voice as soft as the shaving cream she swiped from behind his left ear.

The touch of her finger sent heat ripping through Mallory's body. His fingers closed over hers. "Not much time."

"We should go out. See the area." Eyelids fluttering, she swayed toward him.

He reached out to steady her. That's all he had in mind. Really. The pulse in her neck throbbed like a horse's hooves on race day. When Amy's head tipped up, Mallory read the startled question in her eyes.

Lordy, this is so wrong. The kiss began with sweet surprise but quickly shot into the torrid zone. Amy's lips parted slightly, and his tongue swept in, a honeyed invasion. Startled, she jerked back, body rigid. Heart thudding, he pulled in a breath and waited. Then with a soft moan, she melted into his arms.

"Be a babe." Was that what she whispered?

No time for questions. Amy was so sweet, and he couldn't resist. Her curves filled Mallory's hands as he pulled her closer. His body's immediate response became embarrassingly obvious.

"Oh, my." Voice ragged, she clutched his arms. Were her hips grinding against him a bit? Was that moan coming from her or the rumble of the maid's cart out in the hallway? With those body movements, he picked what was behind Door Amy. But just as he was settling in, she jerked away. Stiff-armed him.

"Oh, I'm sorry! So sorry." Her tangled blonde curls shivered.

"Nothing to be sorry about, Miss Amy." With considerable reluctance, Mallory loosened his hold.

Pressing the fingers of one hand against her lips, Amy looked at him with mute appeal before veering to the twin beds. "Promise me?" Circling back, her gaze clung to him, like she was sliding over a cliff and he was the only one close enough to save her.

Of course." He would have promised anything.

"Promise me that this will not happen again," she said sternly and then seemed to reconsider, lips pouting. "Not today anyway."

Mallory nodded. *Not today?* The gate had indeed been left ajar. And she was being so damn cute about it. "Of course not," he whispered, a thirsty man who'd been promised a drink and still held out hope.

Never had Mallory Thornton had to do more than glance over, and women swarmed toward him like sand gnats in August. But they were all the wrong women. He was rather enjoying this and not in a gentlemanly way.

"The bathroom is all yours." He stepped aside.

"Thank you." As she edged around him, he stifled the urge to kiss her creamy neck.

"I'll meet you downstairs."

With a slight nod, she closed the bathroom door. Were those nude silky things in her hand panties? He sank onto a bed to regroup.

Stifle it, Thornton. Five minutes later, he was strolling down the green-carpeted hallway toward the elevator, but his mind was back in that tiny bathroom, soaping Amy's porcelain back, cupping her curves, feeling her heated body against his and hearing her moan, as she had only moments ago.

He had to get a grip. Stabbing at the elevator button, he broke into a sweat just thinking about her. And he'd just showered. His yellow polo felt damp. Lordy day.

When he got to the main floor, he took his phone from his pocket. Time to give a status report. That might put him back on track.

"We've landed," Mallory announced when Chad answered.

"And she's sending you back to the states, right?"

"My dear man, I am in Rapallo. On the Italian Riviera." Mallory strolled to the door and looked out. "The beach looks fantastic."

"Man," Chad said with an exhalation of breath. "She must really be desperate."

Was Amy desperate? Something was going on, from the looks exchanged by the two sisters. "She's quite a challenge. You probably knew that when you chose her."

"Neither one of us knows that much about her," Chad warned. Now, this was unexpected. "Have fun, but watch it."

"She's a sweet girl."

"Looks can be deceiving. We both know that. Just have fun.

That's the main point. And remember, no flashing of credit cards. No indication that you are Mr. Big Bucks."

"Absolutely. Poor as a church mouse."

What Chad didn't know wouldn't hurt him. Like a Georgia rain shower in July, the remorse washed over him and was gone.

"Want me to come over and chaperone? Mirandah might be up for that." Chad and Mirandah Fairchild had recently become an item.

"Her sister will be doing the chaperoning, thank you very much."

"Her sister is with you?"

"An unexpected surprise." For the time being, Mallory was believing that.

"This could add to the challenge." He could sense Chad's wheels turning.

"With or without the sister, this lady is Mt. Everest." But he wasn't discouraged. Amy was not cold, far from it.

"Keep me posted," Chad said before they ended the call.

Fine, let Chad believe he was working his ass off. Mallory tapped the phone against one palm. What had just transpired in the room had been a game changer. A platonic trip with a travel chum? He wasn't so sure.

Stepping into the small lounge to the right of the reception area, he ordered an Arnold Palmer. The icy lemonade and iced tea might keep his head together, although he certainly would have appreciated the customary sprig of spearmint. Sipping, he considered his options.

The CEO of a major corporation attempting to travel with a woman he didn't know so he could retain his power? His father might have been pleased by his efforts, even if he didn't approve of the method. His mother's assurances that his father loved him deeply never quite softened the jibes Owen Thornton continually threw at his son. Mallory's grades were barely passing throughout his schooling, and his interest in the company never measured up to his father's high standards.

From the corner of his eye, Mallory saw Amy step up to the front desk, wearing a little flowered dress. The short little thing with blue flowers looked light as air, a definite improvement over the bulky safari pants. As she stood there in her brown leather sandals, he admired her legs—shapely and athletic.

He left his half-finished drink on the bar.

"Shall we?" Opening the door, he inhaled her clean, citrusy scent. Rhonda had crowded her dressing table with bottles of outrageously expensive perfume that were all too heavy for his taste.

Stepping out into the sunlight, he adjusted his sunglasses. How delightful. An adventure. They set off at a fast clip, headed for the beach and the bright blue cabanas lining the edge of the narrow shore. As they walked along together, they chatted about the tourist town, shops they were passing, and the parking lot crowded with small European cars. Her enthusiasm was contagious and extended to just about everything.

The sand, the water, the people—she loved it all.

For him, the beach often involved exclusive private homes

perched above an equally private cove. This beach stretched wide, dotted with shaded lounge chairs. Since it was later in the afternoon, parents were packing up beach bags and retreating to their hotels, sleepy children in tow.

The slight squeezing around his heart surprised him. Almost thirty-five, and it looked as if he'd never have this. Picking up the pace, he told himself it didn't matter.

The sandy beach and sea sparkled in the sun. Out in the bay, stately cruisers sat at anchor, rocked gently by the waves. Mallory had seen many stretches of beach, from Brazil to Thailand, but this sure looked like paradise. Amy and her friend must have been planning this for quite a while to get it right.

"Isn't it wonderful!" Amy threw her arms wide.

Smiled at her childlike delight, he eyed the boats bobbing in the bay. "Great place to rent a yacht for a week or two."

Stripping off her sandals, Amy laughed. "You and Daddy Warbucks, right?"

Mallory's chortle fell flat as he kicked off his dockers. Lordy, he had to watch it. What would she think if she knew who he was and how he'd ended up here? The sour taste in his mouth wasn't from the lemonade and iced tea. Scuffing the warm sand under his feet, he followed Amy to the shoreline.

While his travel chum flexed her feet in the sand, Mallory watched the movement of her shapely calves. He pictured her standing demurely behind a desk lecturing to a class about some poet or playwright while she arched upward. Her calf muscles would tense and release, tense and release.

The mental images tensed certain muscles in Mallory's own body.

"Isn't this a great way to start out?" Glancing over, she caught him staring at her legs. "Hello?"

Mallory jerked his head up. "Start what?" That phrase again.

Jerking her head back, she frowned at the horizon. "The trip of course."

Often candid in the way of the Midwest, Amy could also be a puzzle. In Chicago business meetings, Mallory had observed that Midwesterners said what they thought and wanted to get on with it. Must be that cold weather. No use dallying and he was all for it. Sometimes in the South you wondered just what a woman was saying and did she want you to pass the damned butter or not? Phrases like "If I could just prevail upon you" littered the walkway of their words. You had to tread carefully. Not so with Amy. At least so far.

But she could be ambiguous sometimes, and gentlemen did not ask for clarification. At least, not southern gentlemen.

They waded into the shallow water. The underwater sand ridges formed by the rhythmic waves flattened easily beneath his feet. At that moment, everything felt so simple, so refreshing. Maybe Chad had been right. This trip, crazy as it was, might be just what he needed to restore his competitive spirit.

At one point, Amy stumbled and Mallory reached out. She clasped his forearm for just a second, her fingers so delicate against his dark tan. Her tangy citrus scent teased his senses as she fell back against his abs and then pushed away. The imprint of her body tingled, soft and rounded. Damn near took his breath away.

Too soon, they came out of the water. The scent of food curled across the boulevard from the restaurants. Grilling. Olive oil. Fresh bread.

"Let's check them out." He had to think of food to get his mind off Amy Shaw and the fact that she would be sleeping with him that night.

Well, almost.

Chapter 7

The light turned green. Crossing the boulevard was like walking on warm bread. The asphalt had retained the heat of the day and it curled up Amy's legs, invasive and downright arousing. Amy picked up her pace to match Mallory's long-legged strides.

Women's heads turned. The women of Rapallo weren't subtle in attempts to catch the eye of her travel chum. The man was eye candy, no doubt about it. She'd had a fair share of that neck craning when she was with Jason. After all, he was head coach and always gave them a nod.

Mallory kept walking.

When she'd lost her footing on the beach, his chest and stomach had been solid support behind her. She'd been so tempted to stay there, snug against his muscled chest.

Had that kiss in their room made her crazy? She had to think about this. A warning bell went off in her head.

Think about it? That was the old Amy. Might take her a while to let loose. After all, she was a woman without babe experience, not really. In many ways, she felt like a freshman on the first day of school.

"Anything wrong?" Mallory peered down at her.

"Nope, nothing." She followed him into a restaurant. A young man with a broad smile and dark curly hair led them to a table on the patio and handed them menus. After they were seated, Amy's gaze drifted back to the bay, still visible across the busy boulevard traffic. Huge and luminous, the sun continued to slide toward the sea, setting the water afire with a rosy glow. "Will you look at that? Lake Michigan is great, but this, this is exquisite."

"I always enjoy trips to the shore." Mallory opened his menu.

"The shore?" Sounded like something from a travel catalogue. Either Mallory flushed pink or he was sunburned from their short walk. Ducking his head, he nodded. "The Outer Banks. Or Tybee Island. So many wonderful areas, or so I'm told."

"So I'm told," she repeated, clamping a lid on her suspicions. He held up the wine list. "Your pleasure?"

"What?"

With a slow grin, he pointed to the listing. "What kind of wine would you like?"

Holy moly, it was hot in here. "Why don't you choose?"

His gaze pulled away from her like sticky taffy.

Amy concentrated on the menu while Mallory ordered the wine. The man from Savannah sure seemed to know his way around the wine list. They both ordered their entrees.

"The *pollo con gorgonzola* and grilled eggplant sound great," she told the waiter. You were always safe with chicken.

"And I'd like the *saltimboca alla romana*," Mallory said, the entrée rolling off his tongue as if he were ordering a steak with fries back home. Had he said he rarely traveled? What would McKenna say about her constant doubts? She silenced her chattering mind.

66

After the waiter brought the wine, they sat and sipped in silence, although Amy felt jumpy with questions. Why had Mallory chosen this trip? Why he had chosen *her?* But if she quizzed him, turnabout was fair play.

She straightened in her chair. "Wonder where Caitlin and Kurt ended up."

"From the look of the two of them, they won't have trouble finding something to do." Mallory nudged the linen napkin aside in the bread basket and took a slice.

"This is a committed relationship." She hated the prim, defensive note in her voice.

Was it obvious to Mallory that Caitlin was the exciting one in their family? The one who took chances?

"You're lucky to have a sister." Mallory dipped his bread in the saucer of olive oil, swirling it slowly through the dab of pesto at the side. His smile twisted. "My parents had me late in life."

"And do they live in Savannah too?" she ventured. "Your parents?"

"Sadly, they're both gone."

"Oh, I'm so sorry." What would that feel like, losing both parents? "My dad died a while back. My mother can be, well, a little eccentric, but I can't imagine life without her...or my Aunt Em. She moved in with Mom after my father's death."

"Sounds nice, family living together." The note of longing in Mallory's voice pulled at Amy's heart.

"So, there's no one else in your family?"

"Yes. An aunt, an uncle, and the cousin I mentioned."

"That must be fun…a cousin. My aunt never married."

Mallory looked away. "Chad can be crazy, but the man can be fun too." He seemed relieved when the waiter placed a sizzling steak in front of him. Warm juice dripped from the meat, pooling under it like pale blood. Amy's stomach turned. She hadn't eaten red meat in years.

"Certainly beats plane food," Mallory muttered, picking up his knife and fork.

Amy began to cut her chicken breast into substantial squares, her mind returning to an interesting conversation she'd had with McKenna and Nessie about men and their eating habits. They'd were sitting in Petersen's Ice Cream parlor, finishing hot fudge sundaes, when they decided that a man ate with the same enthusiasm he applied to sex. In her limited experience, Amy had found that to be true.

Unbidden, the mental picture of Jason with Greta in the shower swamped her like a tsunami. Maybe *she* was the one who wasn't enthusiastic enough. Her chewing slowed. The chicken formed a dry lump in her mouth, and she wanted to spit it out. Instead, she somehow forced it down.

Across from her, Mallory was taking his time, savoring every bit. Slowly, so slowly.

Amy grabbed her water glass.

"What?" He caught her staring.

"Just, ah, wondered how the steak was."

"Excellent."

Like a lot of the jocks, Jason had been a burgers-and-beer kind of guy. They rarely discussed food. Maybe conversation was lacking throughout their relationship. Why hadn't she noticed that?

Amy sank her fork into a huge chunk of chicken, shoved it in, and swallowed.

The locker room image flashed back.

Everything stopped.

The chicken was stuck in her throat.

She tried to get it down. Nothing. Her fingers fanned out and pressed against the table. Then she grabbed her glass of water.

"Amy?" Mallory looked like he might vault right over the table.

Her heart began to thud heavily in her chest. The sip of water only made her sputter. Her right hand went to her throat. What was the universal symbol for the Heimlich maneuver? How many times had she seen it posted in restaurants?

Mallory's chair scraped back. In two seconds, he was around the table and bending over her. "Amy, can you breathe?"

She shook her head. Little black dots began to appear before her eyes. She struggled to stand up.

Mallory's arms closed around her. "You'll be fine. Try to relax, now."

Relax? Her entire life flashed before her, along with a good dose of regret.

Mallory's chest was against her back. His hands formed a fist below her rib cage. With one movement, he thrust up.

Nothing. Things started to go dim.

Final. This is final.

The other diners' faces blurred to oval pools of light, their expressions ranging from curious to alarmed. She would die, and they would go back to their tiramisu.

"Again." Mallory gave one more firm thrust. The piece of chicken flew out of her mouth and plopped onto the table.

Good grief. Amy fell limp in his arms, like overcooked pasta. Life came rushing back. The tablecloths glowed bright white. The breeze blew soft against her skin. Palm trees rustled overhead.

And Mallory? He was wonderful.

"Take some deep breaths, Amy," Mallory said as she slid down the front of his body and back into her chair. Hovering over her, he handed her the water glass. "Just a sip."

Clasping the glass in both hands, Amy took a small mouthful and swallowed. Her eyes misted over when the water went down. She could swallow. Felt like a miracle to breathe again. Hands still shaking, she swiped at the tears in the corners of her eyes.

Giving her a wary glance, Mallory sank back into his chair.

"Sorry if I scared you." She pushed her plate away.

"Never used that maneuver thing before. It works." Mallory looked pretty pleased. Glancing down, he casually placed his napkin over the piece of chicken.

Amy's attempt at a laugh fluttered at the edges. If she'd been here with Jason, she'd be dead right now. He'd be so busy checking scores on his cell phone, he never would have noticed she was choking. Mallory had been on his feet in a heartbeat.

Putting his fork down, her travel chum motioned to the waiter. "Maybe we should go back. You're a mite pale."

"I'm fine. Really." Her voice felt thin and breathless.

Who would have thought this guy could be so darn nice?

Minutes later, they were walking back along the boulevard. "The bill, we should split it," Amy insisted.

Taking her hand, Mallory threaded it through his arm. "We'll work it out later."

Mallory felt so good, solid and certain, but maybe he was just feeling sorry for her. She hated pity. Pretending to adjust her backpack, she let her hand slip from Mallory's arm. "Usually I can take care of myself."

"I have no doubt."

Amy sniffed, trying to regain her footing. The incident in the restaurant had left her shaken. Close by, waves lapped the shore, lazy end-of-the-day waves. The thought that she'd nearly died rattled her to the core. Made her more determined than ever to live. Really live.

She was going to let loose, try new things and take chances. For one week, she'd be totally not her.

When they finally reached their room, Mallory lounged against the doorframe. "Think I'll go downstairs and have a nightcap. Of course, you're welcome to join me."

Amy stretched her lips into a yawn. "I'm pretty beat."

"I won't be long." As he backed through the door, the lights of the hallway glinted along Mallory's dark hair, his eyes unreadable. Part of her wanted to pull him back, drag him onto the nearest bed and feast on the kind of kisses he'd offered that afternoon.

When had she ever been kissed like that?

The door closed behind him.

Flopping back onto the bed, she inhaled the fresh scent of sheets. She didn't feel at all sleepy and was glad when her phone rang.

"Hey, did I wake you up?"

"Vanessa. Good to hear from you."

"Bo's down for his afternoon nap, and I had to talk to you. McKenna says you've gotten yourself into an interesting predicament." Vanessa chuckled.

"It's not funny."

"Come on," her old friend coaxed her. "I can tell you from experience, take some chances, Amy. And Caitlin's there with you, McKenna says? How bad can this be...a strange man from Savannah?"

"Things aren't bad. They're just surprising."

"Welcome it. McKenna's right. Be a babe."

She thought back to the clothes tucked away in the drawer, the two mini skirts, scooped-neck tops and the sexy aqua sandals that hugged her ankles. All gifts from McKenna. Time to put them to good use.

Everything had been so rushed and confusing before Amy left Chicago that it felt good to catch up with Amy. What a long day. Talking to her friend made her laugh. Vanessa had taken Bo, her toddler, to the park that day, and Amy enjoyed hearing about a misadventure with a drinking fountain that had soaked both of them. While they talked, she cracked open the french doors, and a cool, night breeze from the bay filtered into the room.

After they hung up, Amy dug her pink sleep shirt out of a

drawer and got ready for bed with a hot shower. The warm water soothed her skin but left heated thoughts in her mind.

Being this new Amy, Amy the Babe, was not going to be easy. But it sure as heck was going to be fun. She'd almost died and would have missed all this. Might feel like she was throwing herself from a cliff, but she was going to live.

A nightcap would have been nice right about now. She hadn't come on this trip to go to bed early. What had she been thinking? Time to take some chances.

Chapter 8

The knocking behind her head woke her up. Turning in the narrow bed, Amy cradled the pillow against her left cheek. Was Mr. Morgan in the apartment below working on the plumbing again? A soft breeze feathered across her cheeks. Opening her eyes, she blinked. White curtains billowed from long french doors, giving a glimpse of blue sky patterned by palms.

Definitely not her apartment.

Rapallo. And Mallory.

Amy couldn't even look at the other bed.

Meanwhile, the rhythmic bumping from the next room continued. No mistaking the sound of a couple making love. Amy's stomach constricted with longing worse than her monthly cramps. She rolled flat onto her back. "Geesh."

"Something wrong, Miss Amy?"

"Just Amy." She swung her eyes to the other bed. Babes weren't called "Miss" either.

"Oh, no. You would never be 'just Amy.'" Stretched flat on his back, Mallory grinned, hands clasped behind his head. His long legs were tangled in the sheets. Above that, a pretty spectacular chest was patterned with dark hair forming a sexy downward V. Her gaze lifted to a rakish grin. "Morning, Amy."

"Must be working on the pipes," she offered in a small voice.

If ever a laugh could be southern, Mallory Thornton's was. "Oh, my. I do not believe that sound has anything to do with pipes, at least, not the metal kind."

Periodic moans punctuated the bumping. The tempo had picked up.

Amy fought a giggle. "Probably not."

"Shall we?"

"What?"

"Get going, of course."

"Doing what?" Her hold on the sheet tightened.

"Land sakes!" Her travel chum erupted into laughter. "*You're* the tour guide."

"Oh, that." Amy exhaled. She had to get a grip. Reaching beneath the sheet, she tugged at her pink sleep shirt.

"What don't you go first?"

"Oh, no. I can wait." Her mind leapt ahead. She could dress while he was in the bathroom.

"You sure?" Mallory rolled up, the sheet loose around his hips. The scent of a body warm from sleep rolled over her.

"Positive." Turning back to the french doors, she gave them her full attention. Behind her, she heard the opening and closing of drawers. The minute Mallory shut the bathroom door, she sprang up. While she grabbed clothes, she heard the shower start.

Behind the closed door, Mallory began to bellow, "If our lips should meet, *inamorata*…"

Another one of her favorite Italian love songs. Amy stopped, fresh clothes bunched in her hands. Although Mallory didn't seem to know all the words, his voice sure knew the meaning. And his singing wasn't bad, dipping and expanding in a vibrato that set her own muscles vibrating. She pulled on a mini jean skirt and a pink scooped-neck knit top.

While they traded places between bathroom and bedroom, the two of them talked about visiting the Cinque Terre, a string of hill towns nearby. Amy had a hard time keeping her mind on the conversation. His spicy cologne filled the room, while that buttery accent coated his words. She nudged the french doors wider, trying to concentrate on the wonders of Rapallo instead of the wonder of Mallory Schuster.

Ten minutes later, they entered a small dining room on the first floor. After they were seated, a young waitress appeared with a basket of croissants that smelled heavenly.

Mallory ordered coffee with cream. "Regular, please. I love Italian coffee."

That persistent red flag shot up in her mind. "So, you've had Italian coffee before?"

His face blanked out. "Starbucks. They, ah, often feature Italian coffees. At least, in Sa-vah-an-nah they do."

"Hmm." Amy turned back to the menu. There was something very fishy about Mallory Schuster.

Sunglasses dangling from the front of his pink oxford cloth shirt, he looked like he belonged on the Italian Riviera. High cheek bones flared above freshly shaven cheeks, and she wondered how they'd feel in her cupped palm. Her grip tightened on the menu.

The buffet was simple but ample, and they both decided to try it. Even though this was a vacation, Amy tried to watch her diet. While Mallory piled bacon on his plate along with a couple of hard-boiled eggs and another croissant, Amy poured herself a bowl of granola. They had just sat down again when Caitlin and Kurt appeared in the doorway, hand-in-hand.

Amy waved as the couple walked toward them. Her sister's white shorts and blue T-shirt accented her slim elegance. How could they be from the same gene pool? She'd never worn a single digit size in her life. Suddenly McKenna's pink top felt too revealing.

"Good morning." Caitlin kissed Amy on the cheek. Kurt nodded and pulled out a chair next to Mallory. "How's it going?" Her gaze circled between Amy and Mallory.

"Fine, just fine." Caitlin's curiosity was as subtle as an airport security check.

"Better. I'd say better?" Mallory turned to Amy. "No further problems?"

Confusion clouded Caitlin's face. "What is Malcolm talking about?"

"Mallory," Amy gently corrected her. "Just a small choking incident, that's all."

"You choked?" Caitlin's eyes widened. "Seriously?"

"Shouldn't talk while eating, I guess. Mallory, ah, saved me. I'm fine."

"Didn't Mom drum that into our heads when we were growing up? Do not talk while you're eating. Short memory?"

Amy turned to Mallory, whose lips were twitching. "She did. For sure."

"One of many lessons." Caitlin's attention shifted back to Mallory. "Nice shirt. Not many guys are brave enough to wear pink." Her eyes swung back to Amy. "Matching colors?"

"A gift from McKenna." Amy's cheeks burned. "Most of my shirts are from Caitlin's shop."

"I have a T-shirt shop. *Poetic T's,*" Caitlin explained. "Amy is my walking billboard."

"Well, we'd better move along." Amy glanced pointedly at the time on her phone. Shoot, she sounded more like a drill sergeant than a woman working on being a babe.

In a stage whisper, Caitlin said to Mallory, "Amy likes everything to move right along."

"A point to take to heart." Mallory gave a short nod.

Caitlin shook out her napkin. "She always gets her grades in before they're due."

"Don't I wish." Amy shot Caitlin a look that said *zip it.*

"So what do you guys have planned for today?" Caitlin asked, helping herself to a croissant.

"We're headed to the Cinque Terre, and we probably should get going." But she caught herself up short. After all, Caitlin was here because of her.

"A group of small towns along the coast. Quaint," Mallory said, with enough authority to get Amy wondering again.

"Sounds like fun," Caitlin said, pushing back her chair. "Mind if we tag along?"

'Sure. Why not?" Amy looked at Mallory.

He looked up as he buttered his croissant. "Of course. Y'all come with us!"

His *y'all* wrapped around her like a warm beach towel.

"Great. We're in." Caitlin smiled at Kurt. Pushing back their chairs, they headed for the buffet.

Amy whipped out her travel book and began rattling off the Cinque Terra sites.

"What room are you in?" Amy turned to her sister after the two returned with steaming plates of eggs and bacon.

"324." Caitlin said. "How about you two?"

"326." The sounds from this morning came back to her. Wasn't hard to picture her sister enjoying wild, early-morning sex. Caitlin wouldn't care who heard them.

Did Mallory remember? His grin split wide.

"Okay, we're not spying. It was the only room left." Caitlin's cheeks flushed, like the time she told Amy she'd sold thirty boxes of Girl Scout cookies when Dad had actually bought them.

"Not a problem." Amy began to pick up the croissant crumbs with an index finger.

"So what's it like to be the younger sister?" Mallory asked.

Caitlin threw her head back and laughed. "Not bad. But I was lucky. Last one out, so I was 'Little Dumpling.'"

Cripes. Did Caitlin have to bring this up? Assuming a fetal position under the table seemed like a good idea.

Mallory turned. "And you were..."

"Big Dumpling." The admission clotted in Amy's throat like

one of her mother's hearty German dumplings.

Caitlin fell quiet for a moment. "Daddy didn't mean anything by it, Amy."

"I know." Still, the old humiliation crept over her. Amy felt like the ungainly teenager again. Dad may have meant well, but she'd been relieved when the family dropped the nickname.

Under the table, Caitlin squeezed Amy's hand.

The four of them finished breakfast quickly. When they stopped at the front desk, the concierge gave them information about the boat to Cinque Terra. They were out the door, trotting along the shoreline, where families were setting up for the day. Sure enough, at the end of the cove sat a small stand where a young man sold tickets. Docked at the end of the pier, the boat looked packed. Visitors in sun hats lined the upper railing, cameras dangling from their necks.

The long blast of the horn made Amy giddy as they scrambled aboard. The crew pulled in the plank and let it drop onto the lower deck. One more pull of the horn and the boat edged away from the dock. Leading the way, she dashed up the narrow stairs, Mallory right behind her. "Let's get seats up top so we can see everything."

"Great. We're right behind you." Caitlin and Kurt clambered up after them.

Sun glanced off the water. Gulls circled overhead, crying a welcome. Wasn't this day perfect?

The perfect day to be a babe.

Chapter 9

Mallory tipped his face toward the sun. Lordy, this felt good.

"Will you just look at how beautiful Rapallo looks from the water?" Amy dug into her backpack for her camera. The breeze tossed her curls as they grabbed space on a long bench seat. He liked the natural look. Rhonda had always sprayed her hair into submission.

"No camera?"

He shook his head. "Stopped taking pictures a long time ago."

That first Christmas with Chad's parents, Aunt Sylvia and Uncle Cyrus, had done it for him. What had his aunt been thinking? Hearing her prattle about his mother losing her will to live after Dad's death had done it. No more trips down memory lane for him.

Amy continued to snap photos, enthusiastic as a kid. The women who graced the gaming tables of Monte Carlo and other cities along the coast might be immune to the beauty of the Italian Riviera. It had become wallpaper for them many husbands ago. But not for Amy.

Mallory's eyes shifted to the spectacular shoreline. Craggy trees clung to the steep hills, hanging on for dear life. He'd felt a little like that after his divorce.

How could he execute mergers and acquisitions that leveraged Thornton Enterprises into an international presence that rivaled Bulgari and still be taken in by a woman? The thought dogged him like a persistent hound. Next time, he had to be careful.

If there was a next time. Every man should meet a woman's family before the wedding. He'd been skunked, plain and simple.

As the breeze played with Amy's hair, she pulled some sunblock from her backpack. Watching her apply the lotion to her arms caused every nerve in Mallory's body to stand at attention. Her preoccupied half smile teased him, sexy as all get out. Looking up, she caught him staring.

Jumping to his feet, Mallory shifted his attention back to the water, planting his feet firmly on the deck. The shore was safe.

"How about this sunshine?" he asked, but he still felt off balance. The persistent forward movement of the boat brought other thrustings to mind. Listening to the couple in the other room that morning—the pair that turned out to be Caitlin and Kurt— had just about driven him up the wall.

Amy tapped his arm with the bottle of sunblock. "Want some?"

"Yes…no. I'm fine."

"Okay, but you'll crisp like toast in this sun." She shoved the bottle back in her bag.

"Maybe." Mallory wasn't used to having a woman fuss over him. At first Rhonda had simpered, and then she'd fumed. Finding his footing as he faced the wind, he welcomed the cool rush of air. His travel chum was having an unexpected effect on him.

This was a wager, nothing more. But it was becoming a mite

difficult to keep that in mind.

Sitting down again, Mallory decided he liked being part of this group. As the boat cut through the water, the four of them were rocked into sunlit silence. Not a bad feeling, this family solidarity. Being an only child had certainly not been any fun.

"Look. This must be Vernazza." Amy pointed to a small cove. Amazing how many buildings were crammed along this curved shore. Colorful four-story structures rose from a small square in terraced ridges that gripped sharply angled hills. She pulled a book from her backpack and began to page through it. "There's a wonderful fort in this little town."

"Fort? What about the people? Are they fishermen or farmers?"

"Maybe both. Look." She pointed to the fishing boats pulled up onto the sand like slices of colorful fruit—yellow, red and green. When Mallory had visited the Cinque Terra with some hiking buddies in college, they'd been more interested in Italian wine than the view. Today, he wanted to see what this town was all about. A fort? Not on his list, but Amy kept her finger in the book.

The boat pulled into a short pier. Two crew members jumped onto the dock and began wrapping the heavy towlines around thick white posts. The gangplank slid into place with a resounding thunk. Making their way back down the narrow stairs, the four of them joined the passengers spilling from the boat. The air in the cove smelled of wet sand and fish, overlaid with the tantalizing aroma of early morning cooking. Fanning out, the tourists scattered like ants.

"See you later," Caitlin said as she walked off with Kurt, who slipped one arm around her waist. "We're going to wander around."

Amy watched them leave.

"Want to go with them?" Mallory asked.

Her eyes widened. "No, I'd miss the fort."

Mallory imagined her classroom, every book in its place. But here, why every street led to a new adventure. Amy had pulled the map from her backpack and was turning it this way and that, squinting at the cobblestone lanes that led from the plaza.

"I think the fort is this way." Pointing to the right, she set off like a Girl Scout leader who expected her troop to follow.

"Okay then. See you later." Mallory turned to the left. Shopkeepers were setting out their wares in the early morning shade—fresh produce and flowers to attract the tourists.

"Hey, where are you going?" Amy called. He turned to find his travel chum staring him down. Hands on her hips, she huffed a strand of hair from her face.

"Think I'll see what the locals are up to." He smiled at her above the rims of his sunglasses. "Don't you want to wander around?"

Amy looked over her shoulder toward the street that probably led to the fort. "One of the tour books said the fort's been here for centuries. Don't you want to learn more about it?"

"Learn? Miss Amy, I must decline." School had never been his strong suit. Mallory began to back away.

Arms flailing, she looked positively exasperated, and he fought a laugh. Chad had chosen well. The wager flashed bright in his mind, but he zapped it. He was going to have a good time. But he didn't want her to get lost. "Do you want me to come with you? I think you'll be safe…in the fort."

With a sniff, she dismissed his concerns. "I'll be all right."

Mallory checked his watch. "They said we have an hour."

"Fifty-five minutes now."

His lips twitched as he backed away. "How long does it take to tour a fort?" Sounded about as exciting as watching paint dry.

Her cute nose wrinkle almost made him relent. "Depends on what's up there to see."

Still didn't sound inviting. In Savannah, the squares were filled with wonderful characters. They breathed life into any city. Sucking in more sea air, he backed away. "Later, then."

"Sure. Fine." Turning on her heel, Amy trudged off as if she were on a holy crusade, the backpack pulling at her shoulders.

McKenna would not approve. Amy could hear her friend's advice hissing in her ears. *Be a babe.* But Vernazza held so much history. To ignore it would be criminal.

Amy marched toward the nearest set of stairs that led up and began to take the steps two at a time.

Maybe Mallory was used to taking care of women. Maybe he "saved" them all the time. Her hamstrings stretched as she increased her stride, landing on every other step. Sure, he's saved her at that restaurant, but she could take care of herself.

Distracted, she caught her sandal on a step and went sprawling. The sharp stone edge grazed her shins. A ball of pain, Amy collapsed. For a second she sat there, glad no one had seen her fall.

A tissue or two blotted the blood. Hurt like heck. Standing, she flexed both legs before starting to climb again. Heat ricocheted off the walls with furious intensity. So darned hot and it wasn't even noon.

Stopping to catch her breath, she leaned against a tan stucco wall but quickly pushed away from the burning surface. She needed shade. Above her flapped laundry. Shirts, work pants and skirts hung in the still morning heat, flapping limply every few seconds.

Any breeze seemed so far away.

Maybe she should have stayed with Mallory, where it was cool. Where she could be a babe.

Right now, she was hot, sweaty and bleeding. Definitely not babe material. Shoving off, she began to climb again. Where was the blasted fort? She pictured Caitlin and Mallory somewhere below, seated at a fountain where the air was moist and cool. Maybe they were sipping one of those lemon drinks that were so popular in Italy. Her mouth felt like a cotton ball dispenser.

Amy checked her phone. Only fifty minutes. She kept climbing. When she heard footsteps behind her, she wheeled around, a tactic she'd learned in a self-defense class. A young couple from the ship was taking the steps at a leisurely pace. When the girl giggled, her companion silenced her with a kiss. Amy turned away. Head down, she concentrated on the endless steps.

Was she even headed in the right direction?

When her thighs were burning as bad as her shins, the stairway opened out into an observation area. Up here, the sea breeze cooled Amy's skin. She sucked in the damp air with relief.

Down below, the water sparkled, the deep Ligurian blue that she wished she could capture in a scarf or sweater to have this trip with her always. Wasn't that why she'd considered coming on this blasted honeymoon alone?

To the right, hillsides led down to Vernazza, ringed with walking trails. Olive trees clung to the hillsides. Digging out her book, she began to read until she noticed a group of seniors clustered around a man who spoke in a loud, authoritative voice.

A tour guide. What luck. She inched closer.

"Lookouts would be posted to alert the town." The tour guide swept his hands toward the wall. "You can still see the openings in the brickwork for the cannon."

Amy followed the eyes of the group to the slits in the aged grey brick.

"Over one thousand years ago," he continued, "Turkish pirates would attack Vernazza, sending the women and children running in fear through the narrow streets, searching for a safe place to hide. The men tending the grape vines would rush down to defend the city, but they were, after all, peaceful farmers, not warriors." A dramatic pause allowed everyone to fully appreciate the sad consequences.

Amy gripped the edge of the crumbling stone. What had she been thinking, planning this trip for Jason? He'd never been one for history. When she'd explained the options to him after visiting the travel agent, Jason had nodded, fingering the remote control. "Sure, I like Italian food."

All her idea. And here she was up here, all alone.

Italy was meant to be shared.

She jammed the guidebook back into her backpack.

What was she doing up here by herself?

The young couple came up behind her. A diamond sparkled on the girl's hand. "Oh, Jerry, isn't this grand? Look at this view."

Smiling, the man came up behind her, wrapping his arms around her waist and resting his chin on the top of her head.

A lump swelled in Amy's throat. She glanced around. All couples except for the tour guide, whose wife was probably at home preparing lunch. Sadness engulfed her, and she pulled out her phone. She had to talk to McKenna.

Her friend answered immediately. "Amy? What time is it?"

She glanced at the phone. "I'm so sorry. Almost noon here...so it's five there?"

"No worries." McKenna yawned. "Just got home from delivering a baby. So you and Mallory took a boat trip, huh? That sounds romantic. Where are you now?"

"In a fort."

"Did he drag you there? Sounds like a guy thing and totally boring."

"No, he's down in the town."

Silence was followed by, "Amy, you can always look at pictures of a fort. You are in Italy with a southern hottie. What are you doing right now, lady?"

"The view is spectacular up here."

Amy could hear McKenna's restrained breathing, then a sigh. "Girl, you need some adventure. Climb down out of that damned fort."

"Got it. Maybe I needed a good kick in the pants, as Vanessa's Grandpa Joe would say. What I really need is a cool drink of water and then some wine."

"There you go. Be a babe. Have some wine. Do whatever babes do in Europe."

They said good bye. Moments later, Amy was skimming down the narrow steps, past pink petunias spilling from planters and bougainvillea climbing the cream walls. Her shins stung like crazy.

But she wasn't thinking about her legs.

She wondered what Mallory was doing.

Chapter 10

Mallory strolled inland, nodding to shopkeepers setting out their wares to snag the early morning tourists. A baker was hosing off the stone walkway in front of his shop. The scent of rich earth and fresh bakery filled Mallory with a sense of well-being. Every breath brought him more contentment.

This was really where it all happened. Not the elegant, impersonal boutiques that sold the jewelry he handled.

Worldwide, the Thornton Enterprises jewelry stores made an elegant statement…and were impersonal, he now realized. Maybe he'd have to do something about that.

"*Buon giorno.*" He greeted an older gentleman positioning bouquets of flowers in deep pails in front of his shop.

"*Buon giorno.*" The shopkeeper's leathered skin folded into parentheses around his mouth when he smiled. The few missing teeth only added to his charm. Mallory loved old people. His grandparents had died way too young.

Heaps of colorful fruit and vegetables marked the next store as a grocery. Entering under the bright blue sign, Mallory let his eyes readjust to the dim light. A few shelves held dry goods—cans of peaches, bottles of lotion that could have been there for years. What kind of traffic did this little town have? The top of the wooden counter was scored by decades of transactions. A woman rustled out from the back, drying her hands on a checked apron. "*Signore?*"

"No, thank you." His store of Italian phrases had run out. "Nothing."

Back on the cobblestone street, he caught sight of Caitlin up ahead. She was looking at scarves, holding out the colorful lengths for Kurt to admire. Looked like he was in over his head. Mallory knew how that felt.

"Having fun yet?" Mallory asked Kurt, joining them.

Kurt gave Mallory a wry grin. "Want to buy a scarf?"

"Think I'll pass."

Caitlin folded the lengths back on the table. "Oh, honestly, Kurt, I just wondered which color you liked. The blue pattern or the yellow? You know, to wear over my bathing suit. They're pareos."

"Definitely the blue." Mallory spoke up. "That is, if I could offer an opinion."

Both Kurt and Caitlin turned to him in surprise.

"Why the blue?" she asked.

"It doesn't take a fashion designer to realize that a blue-eyed blonde would look fantastic in blue."

Kurt nodded as if he were taking notes. Mallory wasn't about to mention that his company had several high-end jewelry stores where salespeople often chose gems to bring out a customer's eyes.

Caitlin handed the blue pareo to the young woman who stood waiting.

"Caitlin, mind if I meet you at the boat?" Kurt ran one hand over her shoulders. "I want to check out those fishing boats."

"Not a problem. Don't be late. We'd hate to leave you behind."

They were so darn cute together.

Kurt gave her a quick kiss. "See you there."

Watching Kurt set off, Mallory felt torn. Those boats looked cool. He'd love to talk to the fishermen. But how often would he have a chance to get Caitlin alone?

Caitlin was handing the sales girl a credit card.

"Seems like a nice guy."

"He is. And they don't come along every day. Trust me."

Mallory burst into laughter.

"What?" Caitlin turned to him, her eyebrows rising with that slightly indignant look Amy could wear. The shop girl handed Caitlin her package, and the two of them ambled down the street together, the cobblestones bumpy beneath his shoes.

"Nothing," Mallory said. "Just that you sounded so world weary when you said that and you must be all of…"

"Twenty-five," Caitlin said without hesitation. "Two years younger than Amy and, yes, I've been around the block enough to know that guys like Kurt don't come along every day."

He'd love to be a fly on the wall when Caitlin and her sister discussed men.

"So, I guess you came to surprise Amy when her friend canceled on her for this trip?"

Caitlin's eyes became wary. "Seemed like the very least we could do."

Mallory hesitated. Southern gentlemen did not ask impertinent questions, or so he'd been taught.

"What about you? Why are you doing the Travel Chum thing?"

Ah, the tables have turned. "Guess I just wanted to travel. Break the routine."

"That's it? With a strange woman?" She cocked her head to one side. Lordy, she was as cunning as her sister.

"I can assure you, my intentions are honorable." Partially true.

"Come on. Obviously you're not hard up for company." She seemed to be waiting for an explanation.

Mallory forced a laugh. "My last minute decision was suggested by a good friend. He thought I needed a change." He hoped he looked suitably subdued.

"Aaah." Caitlin's eyes brightened. "Women problems?"

"You could say that. Relationship issues."

"There's a lot of that going around."

"Obviously." Was she talking about Amy? Mallory waited for further details, but the subject seemed closed.

The sun beat down, now almost directly overhead. The cool shadows of early morning had disappeared.

"I'm dying of thirst." Caitlin scanned the storefronts. "Wonder if they have water in any of these stores?"

"Everyone sells water, even in these small towns." Stopping in front of a counter heaped with bananas, oranges, apples and cherries, he carefully tore off a banana and followed Caitlin into the store. Shelves held boxes and cans, but not in massive quantities, like in the states. This was definitely a shop, like the one he'd passed earlier, and not a super store.

To his delight, a box of ginger snaps was shelved among the British biscuits and Italian biscotti. He grabbed one and tucked it under his arm. Best to be prepared. Stomach problems dogged him, and these little beauties always helped.

The shopkeeper quickly stepped behind a glass case holding cheeses along with platters of marinated olives. *"Buon giorno."*

"Buon giorno." Every time he said it, Mallory felt better about this trip. He set his banana and box of cookies on the counter. "I owe you for these."

Caitlin had wandered toward a refrigerated case and slid the door open. "Yep, they have water."

"Get me a bottle, would you please?' Mallory asked. "And probably one for your sister and Kurt."

"You are hungry, yes?" the shopkeeper asked, motioning to the banana and gingersnaps.

"Always," Mallory said. "Is this your shop?"

The man thumped his right fist on his chest with pride. "My shop and my father's too. *Mi famiglia.*"

Smiling at his enthusiasm, Mallory peeled the banana. "I also have a family business."

"You do?" Coming up behind him, Caitlin set the four bottles of water on the counter. "How cool is that? What do you sell…no, let me guess…clothing!"

Mallory shook his head, wondering why in the world she would assume that. He was hardly a fashion plate. "Our largest enterprise involves jewelry."

Now, why had he mentioned his business? Chad wouldn't approve and wasn't he here to forget business? He pulled out some euros he'd gotten at JFK.

Caitlin went for her purse. "Let me take care of it, Mallory."

For the first time, she had his name right.

"Next time." He slid the bills toward the man.

"Caitlin? Mallory?" Amy stood in the doorway, outlined by the sunny street behind her.

"We're stocking up on water," Mallory said, holding up a bottle. "You better get out of the sun."

Blinking in the cool darkness, Amy entered the shop. "I'm fine. The fort was wonderful…so much history."

"What happened to your knees?" Staring at Amy's legs, Caitlin handed her a water bottle.

"I fell, but it looks worse than it feels." Amy held the chilled bottle to her cheek before twisting the top open. Her freckles looked more pronounced across her nose and reddish blonde ringlets formed damp curls on her cheeks.

Caitlin did this *tsk, tsk* thing. "She's very accident prone."

"My, what a display," Amy said, coming closer to the display case. She smelled of the sun and that citrusy perfume she sprayed on herself in the morning. "Not exactly the cold cuts you get back home. Are those…"

"Pigs' feet," Mallory offered. "And tongue, I believe." The plump, fleshy tongue rested beside the cheeses and olives. Probably all local products. Overhead hung shanks of meat alongside plucked chickens.

Amy pressed one hand to her stomach and her attention veered from the tongue. "That cheese looks good." Flushed from the heat, she looked like she'd had a rough morning. Rhonda would be in major whine by now.

With a proud smile, the shopkeeper grabbed one of the yellow cheeses and set it on the counter behind him. A knife appeared, and the slices fell away like butter. Samples were offered all around.

"Hate to leave but time to get back." Caitlin edged toward the doorway.

Mallory raised his bottle of water to the beaming shopkeeper.

"Beautiful," the man called after them. "*Bellissimo famiglia.*"

They definitely were not a family. When the sisters shared a smile, he felt very much like an outsider. What was he doing here? This seemed like a very nice family, good people. Mallory's spirits sank. He could almost hear his father saying, "Son, you are in a heapa trouble."

"Gee, Amy. Your face is so red. Got some block?" Caitlin studied her sister's face.

Amy dug around in that infernal backpack, uncapped the sunblock and began to smooth it on her arms. Again. He wished she'd stop.

"Kurt's down near the fishing boats," Caitlin told Amy. "Wanted to rub elbows with the fishermen."

"What does Kurt do?" Mallory asked as they walked toward the shoreline.

"Websites," Caitlin said with a smile. "Very computer savvy. He'd just finished a project for a major account so he was able to leave at the last minute and the other guys could tweak it. Worked out great."

Mallory didn't miss the look that passed between the two women. When they reached the small plaza in front of the pier, they joined other tourists trailing back to the boat, almost all laden with shopping bags. Waving, Kurt sat dangling his long legs from the wall that edged the beach.

"Hey." He jumped off and walked over. Caitlin handed him the bottle of water. "Aren't you a sweetie?" He bent to kiss her.

Mallory looked away but he noticed Amy did not.

His thoughts zipped back to the kiss yesterday. Funny, but he'd never forget that crazy kiss.

And when Amy raised her green eyes, he knew she was remembering too.

Forget the forts. What had she been thinking? Babes did not hang around crumbling buildings. Glancing at Mallory, Amy felt her lips plump. Was it that crazy kiss in their room only yesterday? The warmth coursing through her veins felt like a raging chocolate fit.

Except now Mallory was the chocolate.

Caitlin and Kurt had already boarded the tour boat, but Amy held back. So hard to leave this all behind.

"Why don't I take your picture?" Mallory asked, coming up behind her. "You'll have something to show your friends."

Wouldn't McKenna and Vanessa love that?

"Thank you." Handing him the camera, she angled herself near a window box filled with purple verbena.

"Say cheese." Mallory worked with the viewfinder and took the picture.

Passing by, an older gray-haired man held his wife's arm to make sure she didn't stumble on the uneven cobblestones.

Mallory turned to the man. "Do you would mind terribly? We would love to have a picture of the two of us together."

Like he read my mind.

Proof of life. Proof of being a babe.

"Of course." The husband took the camera.

"Smile." Mallory pulled her shoulder.

"Beans." She sank into his warm body.

"Oh, Harold. Isn't this sweet?" The wife smiled approval.

They probably thought Mallory and Amy were a couple, just like them.

For this week, they were. Her hands shook as she took the camera. Caitlin waved to them from the top deck, and they climbed on board. The gangplank was pulled up and the boat slowly backed from the pier.

Amy and Mallory found a space up top along the railing. As the shore receded, she snapped photos of the cove and the men working on their fishing nets. The beauty of it all swelled in her throat.

Leaning on the railing beside her, Mallory murmured, "Really a sight. So beautiful, isn't it?"

She sighed. "My thought exactly."

He faced her. "Tired?"

"Just hate to leave."

"Nice thing about trips. You can always return."

Maybe he could. For her? Trip of a lifetime.

They settled onto the bench seat, the wind wreaking havoc with her hair. She didn't care. As the sun climbed, the air warmed battling the breeze skittering over the water. Didn't get much better than this.

Little did she know.

After passing more rugged buttes that dropped to the water, the boat slowly turned into an inlet. Amy jumped to her feet when she caught sight of the cove. And she'd thought Vernazza was scenic. She glanced down at her map. "Monterosso." Even the name sounded beautiful. "Takes your breath away."

"Sure does." But Mallory was looking at her, not the beautiful town lining a breathtaking bay.

Flustered, she peered into the water below. "Isn't this just the most exquisite color blue you've ever seen."

Lifting his sunglasses, Mallory looked down. "The exact shade of a quality aquamarine."

He never ceased to amaze her. "My, you really know your jewelry."

Mallory replaced his glasses with the long fingers that had fascinated her from the start. "The family business includes a chain of jewelry stores. An international chain, actually. My father was very good about giving my mother gifts, you know." Lips tightening, his voice faded off.

"You mentioned your folks last night. Have they been gone long?"

Mallory swallowed hard, and Amy could have kicked herself. "About three years now. My father had a heart attack. My mother died five months later. She just didn't want to be here anymore." The last words were said in an undertone of sadness bordering on abandonment.

Her heart twisted. "Oh, Mallory." She laid one hand on his forearm, warm under her palm. "I kind of felt like that after my dad died."

When he covered her hand with his, the connection felt electric.

The boat slowed and eased into the dock. A rustle of anticipation and everyone was on their feet. An announcement blared over the loudspeaker, telling them to be back in two hours. The staff sprang onshore to tie the boat to anchor, and the ramp clattered down.

Coming up behind them, Caitlin gave Amy a hug. "This boat trip is fabulous."

"So glad you're here, Cait." Her sister could use a vacation, but this trip was probably a sacrifice—all for Amy's sake.

They disembarked. While Caitlin and Kurt took the path that led inland from the dock, Amy and Mallory wandered toward the shops skirting the wharf.

Three-story buildings in pastel pinks, yellows, and blues ranged along the walk with only their colors to separate them. Bright pink and purple petunias jammed window boxes and bordered walks. Overhead, gulls dove when anyone tossed a piece of bread onto the walkway. Perched on a stone wall edging the quay, a group of gray-haired men nodded in welcome, black hats jammed on their heads.

Amy loved it. Excitement picked up her pace, but Mallory didn't seem to be in a hurry, stopping to chat with the older men. Socializing had never been easy for her, but it came so naturally for him. Maybe it was the Savannah thing. With a farewell wave, they finally turned back to the shops.

"How about this?" Bright tops and dresses fluttered from a display. Jason had always hated shopping and refused to even go to the mall with her, although she rarely asked him.

Mallory followed her inside.

Nodding to the woman behind the counter, Amy headed toward kitchen utensils she spotted in the back. Holding up a glass cruet for oil and vinegar, she ran her fingers hands over the cleverly twisted shapes. "This looks hand blown."

Then she saw the dress. Hanging from a hook along the wall, the sea green gown flowed about ankle-length. Diaphanous, it looked as if it had been spun from the waters of the Bay of Monterosso. Tiny mirrors sparkled like pixie dust on the skirt, spraying a dazzling reflection onto walls and ceiling. Amy edged closer. Mallory took the glass cruet from her hands.

"Totally impractical." She had to touch it. Fabric soft as butterfly wings, the material moved with the breeze. Amy swallowed. Oh, yes, this dress would be slinky as sin.

"You'd look good in this." Leaning over her shoulder, Mallory brushed his fingers across the tiny mirrors. She shivered, as if he had stroked her skin.

"So impractical. Where would I wear it?"

"Clothes don't have to be functional. Do they?" Mallory's eyes danced.

Amy gulped. Was this her chance to be a babe?

"Why don't you let me buy you a Travel Chum gift?" he said without even looking at the price tag.

"Oh, goodness no." Snatching the dress, Amy swirled through the shop, the cruet in her other hand.

Babes paid their own way.

With a twinkle in his eye, the shopkeeper rang up Amy's purchases and handed her the prettiest aqua bag. Purple tissue spiked from the top.

Her first vacation purchase. Felt a little wild, a little crazy. She loved it and swung out onto the street feeling pretty pleased with herself.

Outside, Mallory scanned the area. "Hungry?"

"Starving."

"Let's walk." And he took her hand.

Really? "Let's." Tipping her face up to the sun, she didn't pull away.

When had she felt so happy and carefree?

Maybe babes felt like this all the time.

She was going to find out.

Chapter 11

Like some of the restaurants in Rapallo, the walls of Taverna del Corsa were long sliding glass panels that helped cool the interior when pushed aside. Outside, huge hibiscus bushes with platter-size pink blossoms edged the rocks along the shoreline, framing the aqua water below. A waiter seated them at a table overlooking the bay.

As Mallory scanned the menu, the tip of his sunglasses hung from one corner of his lips. Sexy, without even trying.

Mallory looked up. "Everything okay?"

"Fine. Wonderful." *Yikes.* Dropping her head, she studied the parchment listing tucked inside the red leather menu. Thank goodness translations were provided below the entrees. They both ended up ordering the pasta with pesto, a specialty of the area, and a bottle of the local wine.

"The wine of this region is excellent," Mallory began and then clamped his lips together.

Uh, huh. How the heck did he know about wine in this region? Not going to ask. Babes took things as they came. "So, what's it like living in Savannah?"

"Charming." Mallory's smile warmed. "Lots of colorful characters. Wouldn't change one of them."

"You should meet my mother."

His eyebrows peaked.

"Sweet, but kind of eccentric," she supplied quickly. "My father used to call Aunt Emily and my mother Thelma and Louise."

Mallory roared, oblivious to the startled glances from people at the next table. He wasn't a guy who cared about what other people thought. "Now *that* sounds colorful." He wiped the corners of his eyes.

"They are." She smiled, thinking of the fun her mother and aunt enjoyed together.

"Why don't you tell me about Chicago? I've been there, of course, but what is it like to live there?"

She shrugged one shoulder. "Big. Exciting. Lots of history, sort of like Savannah, I suppose."

"A lot bigger. No mobsters in your family?"

"Hah!" she hooted so loud that people nearby looked over. "Is that what the South thinks of us?"

He lifted a brow. "Just asking."

"We're way too boring in Oak Park, although Hemingway grew up there. I went to a Catholic high school, for Pete's sake. The same school where I teach now, as a matter of fact. I'm just a simple West Side girl."

"You seem far from simple, Amy.

"I'm not the type who, you know…" Playing with the salt shaker, Amy searched for the right words.

"Not the type to, what? Sign onto Travel Chums?"

Face flushing, she nodded. "Now that you mention it, yes."

Mallory's blue eyes could sharpen like lasers. "We're here. Everything's great."

"Is it?"

"I think so."

More than great. Much more. Amy shifted her gaze to the bay. The scene resembled one of those TV ads. A couple would be standing in shallow water, oiled bodies beaded with water, arms entwined.

Beaded bodies. For just a second, Amy's mind went back to the locker room. Her stomach heaved, and she launched into more questions about Savannah.

When the waiter returned with a bottle of wine, he presented it for Mallory's inspection. Her travel chum obviously knew his way around wine. Jason would have ordered a beer. The waiter poured, and Mallory sipped. After his nod of approval, the wine was served. A couple mouthfuls and Amy mellowed.

Jason didn't belong at this table. Today, everything was good, and the past belonged in the past. This restaurant was awesome.

Besides, Mallory told great stories and made her laugh. Savannah's music festival and film fest sounded like such fun. Obviously, Mallory was very involved with his city. This trip made her want to travel more, see other places.

Since she seldom drank wine, Amy hated to drink too much on an empty stomach—a rule drummed into her by her mother, along with "never talk while you eat." She alternated sips of wine with gulps from her water glass. Gosh, it was so hot. Perspiration prickled at the edge of her hairline.

Soon the waiter served the hearts of palm salads, followed by the pasta in short order. Savoring her first taste of the rich pesto sauce flavored with basil and pine nuts, Amy looked up.

Mallory was eating again. Her chewing accelerated. Could she stand this one more time? Had she ever heard a man groan with appreciation—just from eating? Mallory brought the fork to his lips with an air of excitement. His eyelids slanted closed for a second as he slowly chewed.

Yep, this was a man who took his time.

With everything? She tossed back her wine. Anything to distract her from the scene across the table.

Where was her mind?

In Babeland.

"The cook has outdone himself," Mallory commented between bites. "I do believe he has."

Dazed, Amy nodded as she sipped, water glass now empty.

The warmth, or something, had stolen her appetite. The breeze that had seemed so cool earlier settled over their table with tented heat. Stupefied, she remained engrossed in the spectacle across the table. Overhead, the whirring fans offered no relief.

"So, do you mind a few questions?" Mallory asked halfway through the meal. "You don't have to answer. Not if you don't want to."

"Not at all." Her tongue felt thick and unwieldy. With great effort, Amy tried to organize the words scattered in her mind, but they skittered away, like the seagulls diving over the bay.

Magically, another bottle of wine appeared.

Setting his fork down, Mallory leaned forward on muscled

forearms patterned with dark hair. She longed to feel their prickly texture on her skin.

Yep. She was buzzed.

A deep line appeared between his dark brows. "Why is a woman like you—educated, attractive—taking a trip alone to Italy, of all places? It's just so romantic."

"I, ah, was planning to come with a friend." At one time, Amy supposed Jason qualified as that. "My friend...Jason." Amy washed his name down with a big gulp of wine.

Mallory sat back. "I didn't know you were involved with someone."

"I'm not. Not anymore."

His blue eyes softened. "Is that what makes you so sad sometimes?"

"Sad? Hard to explain." He'd noticed? Amy stabbed at the pasta, now cool and lumpy, not the warm, buttery dish that had been served. She put down her fork and glanced around.

How she wished she could stay here forever. So romantic. The water. The gulls. The wine. The happy couples around them.

Romance was everywhere.

But not for her.

That's when she started to cry.

While she dabbed at her eyes with her napkin, Mallory set his fork down. "Amy, are you all right?"

"Fine. Just fine." Crunching the napkin in one hand, Amy could not stop the tears. Darn it. How to explain her engagement, the canceled wedding, and the fact that she'd caused the whole mess?

"You're not choking again, are you?" When Mallory leaned forward with a concerned frown, Amy caught a dizzying whiff of cologne mixed with scent of a man who'd spent the morning in the sun. Her head spun. He was more intoxicating than the wine.

"No, I'm fine. Really. More wine, please?" she asked, determined to hold back the tears. This was so humiliating.

Lips pursed, Mallory splashed more wine into her glass. "You don't look fine. Want to talk about it?"

Words wouldn't come. Twirling her wine glass in her fingers, she began to hum one of the Dean Martin songs.

Mallory caught his lower lip between his teeth. "A walk might be a good idea."

"Fine with me." She swung her attention to the bay. The blue water below looked so darn cool and inviting. Plucking at her shirt, she felt wrapped in plastic.

Mallory snapped his wallet shut and circled the table.

When she pushed herself up, her body brushed his and she teetered. Thank goodness his arm shot out to steady her. For a second, they were nose to nose, breathing heavy. Reaching up, she patted his chin. "Scratchy."

"Right." Mallory squeezed her hand and didn't let go.

"Gosh, Mallory, your eyes are like the water." Amy could dive into them.

"Amy, Jason, or whatever his name was, must be an idiot," Mallory murmured as he took her elbow. "I can't imagine a man leaving you."

The wave of sadness felt heavier than the heat. When she

ducked, tears splashed onto her naked left hand.

"That man should be thrashed within an inch of his life," Mallory continued in an undertone, guiding her through the tables.

Amy sniffed. "Do they thrash men in the South? I'll send Jason down." But she couldn't send Jason anywhere, not anymore. And she certainly wasn't about to mention the real reason Jason had dumped her.

After her awkward confession, it shouldn't have been a surprise that he decided the phys ed teacher made a better candidate for Mrs. Jason Hausman. When had he planned on telling her that?

Mallory steered her through one of the low windows that opened onto the bay. Her head felt so heavy, like one of those huge sunflowers they'd passed on the way to Rapallo. Once they reached a bench angled under a tree at the edge of the huge gray boulders, he gently nudged her down. Her body felt like warm taffy, and she giggled. Taffy would just plain melt today.

His hand patted her back. Wasn't Mallory a good guy? "Deep breaths now, darlin'," he said in that low southern drawl that was so reassuring.

"Did you just call me darling?" When she threw back her head, the sun smacked her in the face.

Sitting down next to her, he nodded. "Yes, I did. It's a southern thing."

"That is so sweet." Amy plucked at the front of her shirt. "Let's take a swim."

"Should we?" His blue eyes sparkled.

"Why not?" She kicked off her sandals.

Only took Mallory a second to shed his dockers and strip off his polo. Did they even allow swimming in this bay? He didn't see anyone in the water, just boats farther out. Grabbing her hand, he led her over the stinging hot boulders. At the edge of the rocks, they jumped. The cold water took his breath away, but a sandy bottom met his feet. Not that deep close to the rocks. Laughing, they leaned into back floats.

If this wasn't living, what was?

When he was growing up, he loved trips to Tybee Island. While his mother drove, Aunt Sylvia sat next to her in the front seat of Mom's black Mercedes for the thirty minute ride. Mallory would goof off with Chad in the back. His father kept a condo on the beach, mostly for business. His mother would order a pizza for dinner, something his father hated. They wouldn't head home until it was dark. Sandy and sunburned, Mallory and Chad would fall asleep in the back.

Today the Bay of Monterosso felt just that good.

"Oh, Mallory, isn't this wonderful?" Amy burbled as she struggled to stand, her shirt clinging to her.

He tried not to stare, but she was heart-stoppingly gorgeous and adorable. Tipsy, but her wild abandon added to the fun. Somehow he knew this was out of character and long overdue. When she threw her head back, wet hair fanned above her and then settled into enticing ringlets on her shoulders. He wanted to finger each one. But first he had to get her safely out of that water.

"Isn't this fun, Mallory?" Slapping the surface of the water, she giggled.

"It is. Great fun." He could hardly drag his eyes away from her, frolicking in the shallow water in that little skirt and T-shirt. She looked so happy, like a little girl. Amy deserved a good time. Her story about—what was his name? Jason?—was appalling.

Trailing her fingers through the water, she swung closer.

"Hey, stranger." With a loopy smile, Amy wound her arms around his neck. Every ridge of his body slotted into her curves.

Well, almost every one.

His heart pounded in his chest. Even the chilly temperature of the water couldn't cool his response.

Maneuvering her around in front, Mallory steered her back to the shore. "Careful now," he warned as they clambered over the rocks. Harder to get out than to jump in. They left wet tracks on the boulders as she tipped one way and then the other. He was relieved when they reached the path. One tumble was enough for her today.

"You're so nice, Mallory," Amy whispered, rivulets running off her clothes onto the walkway. He aimed her toward the bench.

An older couple happened to be strolling past. "Are you all right, dear?" the woman asked Amy with a worried frown.

"Wonderful," his travel chum warbled.

The husband raised his brows at Mallory, as if to say *You really have your hands full.*

Not a problem. He was enjoying this.

"Stay," Mallory told Amy after the couple had walked on. He eased her down onto the bench.

Blinking those big green eyes up at him, she grinned. "Yep, okay."

Hiding a smile, he snagged his pink polo and ran it lightly over his torso before tunneling into it. Then he sat down with a sigh.

"Mad at me?" she asked in a forlorn voice. "Guess I had too much wine."

"It was fun watching you enjoy yourself." He pushed a wet curl from her cheek.

"You're so nice, Mallory," she whispered right before her mouth slid onto his. Her lips felt incredibly soft.

"Yummy." Amy giggled against his mouth. Her tongue darted out to trace her grin, sweeping his in the process.

"For starters," he muttered.

"Uh, huh." She nodded, eyes already closed tight as they dove into another kiss. Her mouth gently opened, and his tongue explored. Her soft moan just about undid him.

How much time passed before he felt someone watching them? Caitlin and Kurt stood taking this all in, curious smiles on their faces. He straightened. *PDA.* He'd never gone for public displays of affection, but this was different. Amy was different.

"Hi, sweetie!" Amy smiled up at her sister, never loosening her hold on Mallory's neck.

"Having fun?" Caitlin wore a small, bemused smile.

"You bet."

"Everything okay?"

"She's fine. Your sister's just fine." Running his tongue lightly over his lips, Mallory gently worked his arms free.

"I went swimming," Amy explained, combing one hand through her wet curls. "Cait, I just let loose."

A bit of an understatement.

"I guess so." Apparently, Caitlin found this highly amusing.

Behind them sounded the deep warning horn from the boat.

Grabbing bags and belongings, the four of them scrambled toward the dock. With Amy's packages and backpack looped over one arm, Mallory steadied her with his other hand.

A motley crew and he didn't care. The imprint of Amy's lips throbbed. He wanted more.

So hard to remember that this had all started with a wager. Way before his travel chum materialized as Amy Shaw. Sure, this trip could solve a lot of problems for him with his board. Only now, the travel chum was a person…with a family. He didn't want to hurt Amy in any way, especially since hearing that sad story about some idiot named Jason.

The sweet teacher was getting to him.

And today was only Monday.

Chapter 12

As the tour boat approached the dock, Rapallo glowed in a golden light. "How beautiful," Amy sighed.

Mallory nodded, the setting sun burnishing his features.

Today had been amazing. Her lips swelled remembering that kiss. Dazed and content, Amy followed Mallory down the gangplank. The new shirt from McKenna felt like it had shrunk. She loved it. Up ahead, Kurt and Caitlin ambled toward the boulevard, his arm around her waist while she rested her head on his shoulder. Caitlin had always been a cuddler. Amy, not so much.

Not until Mallory.

"You should do this more often," Caitlin had whispered while they sat on the upper deck of the tour boat.

"Oh, Caitlin. I blew it." Amy dropped her head into her hands.

With a pleased grin, Caitlin bumped her shoulder. "Not at all. Didn't I tell you to let loose? Mission accomplished, girl. You rocked it."

As the four of them straggled from the boat, evening was falling. Couples sat at intimate patio tables, sipping wine or lingering over coffee. Wiped out, Amy thought longingly of the crisp white sheets on her twin bed. She could sort everything out tomorrow.

She could plan how to let loose, without letting go. Amy gave her aqua bag a little swing. Mallory whistled softly as he strolled along beside her.

"You must think I'm an idiot," she said softly.

"Why would you say that?" Mallory stopped, one hand taking her elbow. Heat radiated from his touch.

"I must seem like some ninny who can't eat without choking or drink with moderation." Embarrassment brought the fingers of one hand to her lips, where the impression of his kiss still pulsed.

Had she really mentioned Jason? At least she hadn't blurted out the whole horrifying story.

"Look at me. Please." Halting, Mallory tilted up her chin.

What she saw in his face sure looked like understanding, not disgust.

"You are having a rough time right now, Amy. I get that. I do indeed."

"You are so nice, Mallory."

When he ran a thumb pad gently over her lips, she shivered. Then he grinned, his crazy, boyish smile that made him look sixteen. "I did have a fine time with you today."

"You did?" Her laugh bubbled out on a wave of surprise. If only McKenna and Vanessa could have seen the two of them jumping into the water.

"Nothing wrong with an impetuous woman." His lips twitched.

Impetuous? She liked it.

Their pink stucco hotel lay just ahead. A night breeze rustled the palms overhead, bringing the pungent smell of the sea. Caitlin and Kurt had disappeared, and Mallory pushed open the glass door. Amy stepped into the cool air of the foyer.

"Why, Miss Amy, I declare. You should let yourself go more often," he murmured, breath warm on the back of her neck.

When they reached the room, Amy disappeared into the bathroom. Mallory stepped out onto the balcony. Traffic whined below and diesel fuel hung in the cool night air, but the sparkling lights of Rapallo weren't on his mind. No sir. Nothing could eclipse the memory of Amy rising from the aqua waters of the Bay of Monterosso like some mythical sea nymph.

How had this happened? His cousin had stumbled onto some website, and he'd met this woman?

Suddenly, all things felt possible. Her transformation that afternoon had been downright amazing. And that kiss? He ran his tongue lightly over his lips to revive her taste. He wanted much more of Amy Shaw.

Here under false pretenses, he was embarrassed to admit how much he enjoyed spending time with her. Her impulsive streak fascinated him. Rhonda's kisses, he realized too late, had been the practiced result of much experience.

Amy's kisses felt soft and vulnerable, like a surprise gift she wasn't sure he wanted.

But he did.

Caution squeezed in his chest. Was the Chicago school teacher just another Rhonda, out for what she could get? When he'd mentioned Thornton Enterprises, she didn't bat an eye. Obviously she'd never seen their name on the Yahoo finance page.

Behind him, the bathroom door opened, and he turned. Amy's eyes widened as if she were surprised to find him there. Her glance slid to her bed with undisguised longing.

Great. So he was back to being just her travel chum. The guy sharing her room. "Think I'll get something to eat after all. Anything for you?" Making tracks toward the door, he drummed an impatient path across the dresser with his fingertips.

"Think I'm going to turn in." Those sun-tinted cheeks and freckled nose—she was adorable. Restless warmth stirred in his body.

"See you in the morning, then." He backed away, wishing she'd say, "No I'll come with you" or "No, stay."

But she didn't. At a loss after he'd closed their door behind him, he called Chad.

"So, how's it going?" boomed his buddy. "Are we having fun yet?"

"We're, ah, getting physical."

"The teacher? Are you serious?"

The vision of Amy rising from the bay remained branded in Mallory's mind. "Trust me, teachers can certainly be surprising."

As he leaned against the wall, phone to his ear, the door of the next room opened, and Caitlin and Kurt emerged. "You and Amy heading out to dinner?" Caitlin asked, looking very pretty in a blue sundress with some sort of a ruffled skirt. All women should wear ruffles.

"Right, I'll get back to you in the morning with a decision."

Mallory switched to his usual CEO voice before pocketing the phone. He pivoted toward Caitlin. "Your sister's plumb tuckered out."

"What?" Caitlin aimed a disgusted look at the closed door. "Want to come along with us for dinner?"

Her boyfriend nodded. "Sure. We're just headed out to the boulevard."

"That would be great, if y'all don't mind." He sure as hell didn't want to go out alone. Amy's sister and her boyfriend seemed like good people. Hells bells, they had no idea he was Mallory Thornton, and even if they heard his name, it probably wouldn't amount to a hill of beans with them.

His newfound anonymity felt freeing.

"You two go on, and I'll meet you in the hotel lobby, okay?" Caitlin positioned herself at Amy's door.

Kurt and Mallory locked eyes.

"Girl stuff," Mallory said in an undertone. "Let's get a beer."

They walked toward the elevator. "Don't be long, Cait, okay? I'm starving. We'll be in the bar," Kurt threw over his shoulder.

Caitlin was already pounding on the door.

Appreciating their dinner invitation, Mallory was determined that he would mine Caitlin and Kurt for information. What could it hurt?

He'd become very curious about Amy. An evening with a close source could provide answers.

"Did you forget something?" Amy asked, yanking the door open.

"Yes, you." Caitlin burst in, slamming the door behind her. "You're staying in? Why?"

Amy plunked down on the bed. "Cait, I have to get it together."

"Mallory's hot and obviously into you." Caitlin frowned. "And he's fun. A lot more fun than that idiot Jason."

Amy sized up her sister. "Caitlin, Jason had a reason for being an idiot."

Her sister frowned. "No engaged man can be excused for jumping into the locker room shower with another woman. The guy's an idiot."

Amy sighed. "The night before the locker room fiasco, I told him, well, that I could never have children. Jason was pretty unhappy. This is a guy who comes from a family of five boys."

"All of them morons," Caitlin mumbled under her breath while her frown deepened. "What are you saying? Of course you can have children."

"Caitlin, remember all those painful monthly periods? The ones that kept me home from school, huddled in bed?"

Sitting down, her sister took Amy's hands. "Yeah, you had a hard time with endometriosis, right? But Dr. Jenson did that procedure."

"It came back. Worse than ever. Messed everything up." Tears thickened Amy's voice. "I should have told Jason sooner, but I just couldn't. Dr. Jenson was painfully blunt. I couldn't lie to him about it."

For a second, Caitlin's face went blank. "Dr. Jenson delivered us, Amy. He's an old man now, maybe not up on the latest medicine. Let's check with another specialist."

If a cloud drifted over Caitlin's horizon, it always had a silver lining.

"I like Dr. Jenson." They had never agreed about their mother's doctor, but maybe Caitlin had a point..

Wrapping her arms around Amy, Caitlin planted a kiss on her forehead. "You'll see. We'll find a wizard to fix it." As children, *The Wizard of Oz* had been their favorite movie. "Mallory's ten times the man Jason is. Enjoy him."

"He's just a traveling companion."

Caitlin frowned as she swept the twin beds with a disapproving glance. "Amy, adults don't have traveling companions that look like Mallory."

"I'm not his type."

"How do you know? Kurt and I are headed to Florence tomorrow but let's not make this a group excursion," she said pointedly. Jumping up, Caitlin stared Amy down.

She got the message.

So she was on her own with Mallory?

"You are not the poor rejected bride. You're an adventurous, hot woman. I think you're in safe hands. Now work it." Caitlin grinned.

"Oh, Cait. Do I even know how?" Amy thought back to the thumping on the wall that morning. Her sister obviously knew how to "work it."

"Of course you do. Mallory was devouring you with his eyes on that boat trip. You could have won the wet T-shirt contest today, hands down. And the short skirt? I won't even go there."

Playing with one of her frizzy curls, Amy blushed.

Springing to her feet, Caitlin reached back for one more hug. "This week is a gift, a one-week gift. Why not open it? We need to find another doctor for you, Amy, but not this week. This week, just pretend you're someone else."

Someone like Caitlin, Amy thought to herself as her sister swirled out the door in her sundress. Those ruffles sure looked pretty.

Maybe she should consider some ruffles. But she had that blue-green dress. Where would she wear it first—Florence or Venice?

Chapter 13

They were headed for Florence. Mallory had a lot on his mind after dinner with Caitlin and Kurt.

"Mallory, I am so sorry about yesterday." Amy had been subdued at breakfast.

But he didn't want an apology. Feeling like a palmetto bug squished beneath the wheel of the rental, he squirmed in the bucket seat. "No need to apologize."

She gave her head a saucy shake. "Good. Then I won't."

How he wished he could read her like the guys in his poker group. At some points, he thought he knew just where her head was. But not always. This might be a hand he'd never played. "Hate to bring this up, but it could have to do with the cad who decided not to accompany you on this trip."

"Maybe." The sun beamed through the front window. Amy brought out her bottle of sunblock. "You don't have to take care of me on this trip."

"I'm not complaining," Mallory insisted. Good God, not easy to keep his eyes on the road. He wanted to be her hand—traveling up and over that soft skin. After yesterday, he knew how that skin felt. Silky. Mallory tightened his grip on the steering wheel.

"Your profile said you were divorced."

"That would be correct." What else had Chad mentioned?

"Did you take care of your wife? Just tell me if I'm being too personal."

Remembering never got easier. "When I actually got to know Rhonda—which unfortunately was after the wedding—care and concern weren't what she wanted from me."

"Oh, dear." Amy brought one hand to her chest.

What had they been talking about?

Oh, right, his short and ugly marriage.

"Rhonda may have been very independent. Women can be like that, you know." Definitely a defensive tone in Amy's voice.

Was she talking about Rhonda or herself?

"My ex was used to being on her own. She had a lot of responsibility with her job." He paused, edging close to an admission that came with a whole boatload of pain. "But it wasn't her independence that drove her into the arms of Raoul, the tennis pro at our club. Just a matter of habit with her, I'm afraid. By that time, we both realized that this had been a mistake. It was a very short marriage."

"Oh, my." Amy's hand tightened on her shirt. Downright distracting.

"My poor judgment." He was determined to count to ten before he glanced over again.

"So you just divorced her?"

"Our parting was somewhat consensual."

"You mean you changed your mind?" Amy asked, her voice a soft whisper.

"It happens." Mallory shifted in the seat. Now, if he were seated in his board room, he would simply move to the next agenda item.

Was she aware that her nipples were quite pronounced with her hand tight on that damn shirt? She wasn't the type of woman who'd try to produce this effect, this much he knew. The pads of his thumbs began to tingle.

Good God, he needed a cold shower. Hunched over the wheel, Mallory drilled his eyes onto the road in front of him, grateful that he wouldn't be expected to stand up for some time.

After a while, Amy dozed off, giving him a chance to see what their rental car could do on the road, which wasn't much. Pretty soon, he'd have that specialty model of Chad's and he could play with that on a highway, although certainly it wouldn't be in Italy.

Funny, the thought of that "prize" wasn't as exciting as it had been two days ago.

He adjusted the sun visor to give Amy some shade. Curled up next to him with one hand nestled next to her chin, she looked like she was sixteen.

Cars. Concentrate on your collection, you idiot.

Jerking his attention back to the road, he mentally catalogued the contents of his garage in Savannah, beginning with his Jag and ended with the Rolls Royce he used for touring clients. The Rolls had belonged to his father, which in itself was reason to get rid of it, but for some reason, he kept it.

The miles fell away as the sun climbed high. Opening a window, he was so damn glad he'd listened to his cousin. Well, part of it. His mind turned to Thornton Enterprises and the rollout for his latest acquisition. For the past two days, he'd been exchanging calls with Miriam. As usual, she had things well in hand. The business deal could wait. This trip and its outcome were more important.

Strangely, this no longer felt like business.

Although he was holding himself in check, he was beginning to think she might be the real deal—a woman with scruples, a woman who didn't lie.

But wasn't he doing just that? Queasiness seized his stomach, and he wondered about the scallops he'd ordered the night before.

Damn this heat. Closing the window, he flipped on the air.

Had Amy's story and her obvious distress side-tracked him? As with any business proposal, Mallory wanted to remain objective, free of any emotion that could skew his judgment. He was having a hard time doing that with Amy.

Why couldn't he control the air in this car? Rolling down the window again, he inhaled the passing fields. Even enjoyed the smell of diesel fuel that was so European. Today he was feeling happy as a clam at high tide, well, except for his back. After two nights on that twin bed, his back was killing him, a disadvantage of being tall. He hoped to work that out in Florence.

Everything was possible. Wasn't that what had earned him his success? He began to hum "Volare," one of the songs that kept trailing through his mind.

Mallory didn't know how much time had passed when the exit to Florence came up. In the noonday heat, traffic slowed to a crawl through narrow streets. Thank goodness, the car, modest as it might be, came with a GPS system, and he tapped in the address of the hotel Miriam had booked. No more small, spare rooms that reminded him he was supposed to be on a travel budget.

Somehow he had to make this switch to an upscale hotel acceptable. Not easy since Amy was one independent woman. She had to accept what he was doing or she'd never accept him.

Passing over the Santa Trinita Bridge, he drank in the weathered stone buildings, the bustle of people chattering in other languages, the sparkle of the Arno River—why hadn't he done this earlier? Of course, the only interest Rhonda would have had in Italy would be the Milan fashion shows. Amy didn't seem to give a rip about clothes. And yet, she'd sure liked the long blue dress in the shop.

A woman with no interest in designer clothes. He liked that.

Pulling up in front of the Hotel Helvetia & Bristol, Mallory gently shook Amy's arm. "We're here."

Stretching, Amy squinted out the window. "Where are we?"

Rocketing upright, she blinked and then started rummaging through that infernal backpack, bringing out the folder where she kept all her paperwork. He held his breath. Darting a suspicious look in his direction when a doorman bustled out to open her door, she clutched the folder to her chest. The doorman froze.

"I, ah, have a surprise for you." Mallory worked to inject just the right amount of doubt into his voice. "After your, well, difficult time in Rapallo, I felt I owed you a treat. I hope you're all right with this change."

Amy's head craned upward, taking in the impressive stonework. "You shouldn't have done this." But she was smiling.

Springing from the car, Mallory tossed the keys to the doorman, who nodded and opened Amy's door. They were going to have a fabulous time. He would see to it. Soft silk comforters, heated towels, and spray jets strategically placed in the Jacuzzi—they could make progress here.

Stepping out onto the sidewalk, Amy stumbled and he caught her, steering her through the entrance. With every step, her eyes grew wider.

"My word, Mallory. Have you robbed a bank?" She scanned the lobby.

"Not yet." He looked around. Yes, this hotel would do nicely. The marble topped tables, original artwork and elegant sitting areas spoke of good taste. His shoulders unwound and the ache in his back eased.

But he could tell he still had some selling to do.

"Caitlin would love this place, wouldn't she? My word, think of the stories you'll have to tell your family." Mallory's dinner with Caitlin and Kurt had been extremely helpful. Very apparent that Caitlin may have been indulged all her life, while Amy was the responsible one. By the time they were laughing over coffee, he'd clearly identified his opportunity. A tiny smile bloomed in the corners of Amy's mouth. "Wouldn't this just drive Caitlin crazy?"

"Sure would. Why don't you wait over here." Mallory led her to a damask chair.

Amy sank onto the cushions, one hand stroking the rich fabric, while he turned to handle check-in. Moments later, they were on their way to the room. When the porter pushed open the door to their suite, Amy was practically speechless. "Oh, my."

Miriam had done him proud. She excelled with details. The suite was decorated in shades of moss green. Although it had pained him, he'd given his assistant instructions to request twin beds. And yet, he was beginning to hope they might have need for a queen, at the very least.

There they sat, two single beds, which would not advance the plan building in Mallory's mind, but he'd just have to work around them.

"Oh, Mallory." Stepping to the window, Amy gazed out over the rooftops of the city. "How breathtaking." Like a small child in a toy store, she inspected everything thoroughly, pushing back the heavy drapes, opening and closing drawers and doors. She practically skipped into the bathroom while he lounged on the nearest bed. Thank God for firm mattresses.

"Will you just look at this?" came the yelp from the bathroom. "A marble Jacuzzi!"

Breathing a sigh of relief, Mallory figured they had moved beyond the deciding point. He began to unpack, listening to Amy sing to herself as she darted around the suite like a humming bird. The situation was just so domestic. Her soft, feminine things filled the room—the citrusy perfume, the brushes, combs and makeup bag she stacked on the glass shelf next to the sink in the expansive bathroom that offered every luxury.

He hoped they'd use every one of those amenities.

"What now?" When she'd finished arranging things with her customary sense of order, she pulled her map and travel book from the backpack.

"Explore after we clean up?" Peering down from the window, he tried to figure out where they were. As much as he would have loved to while away the afternoon conducting an exploration of an entirely different sort.

"Sounds good." Amy stayed glue to her map.

Now for that cold shower.

A little later, he took care of some phone calls while she showered and changed into her mini skirt with a pale pink top. Her hair was caught back in some kind of clip that, thankfully, didn't hold. Curls escaped and tumbled to her shoulders.

As they exited the elevator, Amy chattered about the art collections in the Uffizi. The world-renowned museum apparently was on the schedule for tomorrow. Two women stood at the reception desk and Amy's steps slowed, her excitement replaced by a puzzled stare.

"Gosh, that woman looks like my mother from the back," she whispered. "And the other lady… Wait a minute."

He took her arm. She damn near looked like she might faint.

"Is that Aunt Em?" Her tone had turned from mild observation to shock.

First Caitlin, now her mother and aunt? Had this been in her profile?

Mallory and Amy approached the desk just as the two women turned. "Mom?"

The redhead flung her arms wide. "Honey, we were just asking if you'd checked in yet."

"What are you doing here?" The color had drained from Amy's

face. "And how did you find me?"

This family was simply amazing—but fun.

Ducking her head, Amy's mother fussed with the back of her hair, eyes sparkling with mischief. "Caitlin. I just gave her a call. Boy, was I ever surprised that she was here in Italy. You girls. Imagine that!"

Amy looked totally panicked.

"I may have mentioned this hotel to Caitlin last night during dinner," he admitted.

Amy's poor mother squirmed. "You see, Em and me, well, we just thought we should be here for you. We didn't know Caitlin was coming with Kurt until we called her yesterday. Those stinkers!" She flashed a sassy grin. Mallory liked her immediately.

"Right. Very sweet." Amy managed a daughterly hug, disbelief frozen on her face like the first winter frost on the marshes.

Still, pretty graceful recovery. One stunt like this and Rhonda would have handed her mother's head to her on one of Mallory's silver platters.

"See, I told you Amy would be tickled to see us." Her mother smiled at her companion, who must be Aunt Em. The delicate older woman with faded blonde hair threw a questioning glance his way.

Mallory stepped up without hesitation. "Ladies, I'm Mallory. So pleased to meet y'all."

Chapter 14

"Mallory, my travel buddy." Amy's voice wobbled. Was this really happening?

"Mallory." Mom tasted his name, savoring it like the fudgesicles she loved on hot summer days.

Mallory placed a hand on Amy's shoulder, the warmth of his hand radiating through her body. "Travel buddy or travel chum. So very happy to meet Amy's family."

Aunt Em stepped closer. "Are you from a foreign country?"

"Sa-va-yah-nah," Mallory answered with obvious delight.

Exasperation swirled through Amy like the wind tunneling between Chicago's skyscrapers. Wasn't this the pity party she'd wanted to avoid? Still, she was touched. "Mom...Aunt Em, I can't believe you came all this way for me."

Louise's smile froze. "Are you mad, honey?"

"Just very surprised." Amy chose her words carefully. Wasn't it enough that she'd disappointed her mother by calling off her wedding? Not that her mom blamed her after what had happened, but she'd been so quiet when they'd talked over the phone. Leaving Caitlin, McKenna, and Vanessa to handle the details of the canceled wedding, Amy had pretty much gone into hiding. Once she'd been matched up with Mallory on Travel Chum, she'd told her mother only that she'd found someone to accompany her to Italy.

Never in a million years would she have dreamed her family would come all this way for her.

"You didn't tell us your chum was…you know." Her mother's eyebrows lifted.

"I didn't know Mallory was a man."

"Oh, my goodness!" Aunt Em clapped one hand to her mouth.

"An honest mistake, I can assure you." Mallory's Savannah-sugar voice rippled with suppressed laughter.

"We thought we'd surprise you," Mom said with a sheepish grin. "You know, when things didn't work out. Emily and me, well, we've never seen…Tuscany." The last word was uttered with childlike wonder that made Amy smile.

"You'll love it, Mom. Really, it's great that you came." But this family thing was very weird—like holding a family holiday in another country.

Mom darted a furtive look at her sister. "You know, it all happened so fast. Caitlin and I talked, but we like to keep out little secrets."

"Right, we didn't want to tell anyone," Aunt Em chimed in, as if this was the naughtiest thing in the world.

"When I called Caitlin yesterday to see where you were staying," Mom continued, "I couldn't believe it when she said she was over here. Boy, was she ever surprised that we were coming." Her girlish giggle was full of mischief.

"Surprises are such fun." Aunt Em's nose wrinkled.

"As I leave and breathe, absolutely delicious," Mallory drawled.

Amy looked from Mallory to her mother and aunt. Excitement quivered in the air. This might be more fun than any wedding. "Caitlin mentioned they were in a hotel near the river. You know she's with Kurt."

Mom's shoulders came up. "Well, of course, dear. You think I'm not a modern woman? I know about these things." She circled one hand between Mallory and Amy.

Frustration knotted in Amy's stomach. "Mom? We are *not* one of those things. "We're just…""

"Travel chums," Mallory supplied with a devilish grin. "Seeing the sites."

Amy nodded, staring him down and slipping her shoulder out of his grasp—even though it had felt so good. "Exactly. Just sharing expenses…and stuff. This hotel came as a total shock." The exquisite lobby mocked her words.

"I did take the liberty of making this slight change to Amy's itinerary," Mallory murmured.

"It's dandy." Mom's eyes swept the high ceilings.

"My, oh, my." Aunt Em looked equally impressed, one hand on the elastic waistband of her navy slacks.

Amy's knees felt weak. "I think I need some food."

"Me too!" Mom piped up, glancing down at her sturdy white tennis shoes. "Where to?"

"Why don't we take a stroll? See what the city has to offer," Mallory suggested, ushering them toward the door.

Outside, sunshine reflected off the stone buildings along the

Via del Pescioni, bathing the street in a golden glow. Compared to the busyness of the beach in Rapallo, the area felt stately and sedate—bushes trimmed, the flowers properly bedded. Within moments, the four of them turned onto a more congested avenue. Tourists clutched maps and cameras, craning their necks and consulting guidebooks. The pace picked up, and the air filled with honking horns and the rumble of traffic.

The narrow sidewalk confined them to walking two-by-two, and Amy fell back with Aunt Em. Staying close behind her mother and Mallory, she struggled to catch snippets of the animated conversation. She wanted editing privileges.

For once, her mother was talking in an undertone, Mallory's head bent close. Was her mother going to reveal that Amy had always cleaned her plate, that Mom tried to persuade Tommy Taylor, the grocery delivery boy, to take Amy to Senior Prom?

Exhausted, she finally fell back.

"Everything okay, chickadee?" Aunt Em patted her hand.

Amy smiled at her childhood nickname. Aunt Em had never called her Big Dumpling. She'd always been her aunt's little chickadee, first in the nest and maybe a favorite.

"Everything's fine," Amy assured her aunt, taking her arm. Recreating herself as an adventurous woman might be harder with her mother, aunt, and sister in tow.

"Like your hair." Aunt Em took in Amy's new highlights with appreciation.

"Got it done before, well, the trip." "Honeymoon" had nearly slipped out.

Up ahead, Mallory still hung on Mom's every word. Had her mother ever had such a devoted audience?

"My, he is a fine specimen of a man," Aunt Em whispered.

"Yes, he is." Mallory's broad shoulders filled his yellow polo. His longish hair lifted on a hot city breeze.

The kiss in Monterosso came back, shivery and sweet.

"What's he like?" Aunt Em leaned closer.

"He's been...a decent guy."

The Bay of Monterosso? Not decent, thank goodness.

"And you're, you know..." Her aunt's face colored.

"Roommates. That's it, Aunt Em. Two can travel cheaper than one. But then Mallory surprised me with this room. Outrageous really." Words fast and crisp, she was babbling and clamped her lips firmly shut. This situation was crazy, but she'd probably never stay in a room this elegant. Caitlin would be wild with envy.

That thought gave Amy enormous satisfaction.

Outside one open shop door, long aprons fluttered from a circular rack. The huge yellow sunflower on white cotton with "Firenze" scrawled across the bottom caught Amy's eye. She had to have it.

"My daughter's a terrific cook, you know," Mom told Mallory when Amy stopped to make the purchase.

"I didn't know that." Mallory's gaze brushed Amy.

"Her popovers are to die for." Louise smiled proudly.

Amy yanked her wallet from the backpack. "Mom, really. I'm sure Mallory's not interested."

His blue eyes sparkled. "Oh, but I am. Popovers? Light and

puffy, with warm butter melting slowly into the crevices." Mallory's full lips came together as if he were tasting one.

"Pockets. They're pockets of air." Amy crushed the apron in her hands. "In the popovers, I mean."

"Gonna buy that, sweetie?" Louise's eyes danced between Amy and Mallory.

"Yes, right." Quickly Amy handed the apron to the sales clerk and paid.

After she squashed the bag into her backpack, they continued their stroll through city central. The scent of grilled food hung in the air and vendors beckoned from doorways. At one point, they passed a jewelry shop and of course Louise had to venture in, Aunt Em trailing behind her.

Staying outside, Amy felt she had to explain. "I didn't know they were coming. Really."

"Well, now, did I say this was a problem?" Looking pleased, he folded his arms over his chest, as if he were the official guard for the group. "Your family might be a rare treat. Yes, indeed."

Head bobbing, Mom held an animated conversation with the shopkeeper, who dangled a pair of gold earrings from one hand.

"Mom and Aunt Em have a jewelry business. They work out of the house and sell their designs at art fairs and local salons, that kind of thing." That meager income had been so welcome after her father's death.

Mallory's eyebrows peaked. "You'll have to show me their work."

Her mother had turned from the counter, shaking her head as

she came back outside. "Tricky designs. I had some questions."

"Louise, I think he was flirting with you," Aunt Em giggled. Amy's mother flushed with pleasure.

Over the tops of his sunglasses, Mallory's gaze met hers as if they shared a wonderful secret. Jason's kisses hadn't excited her as much as Mallory's glances.

The thought stopped her in her tracks.

"You okay?" Mallory pulled up beside her. Mom and Aunt Em were looking at table linens displayed in a window.

"No. Yes. Of course." Picking up the pace, she put one foot in front of the other, but she couldn't outdistance the realization that she almost married a man who didn't excite her, not really.

"I'm hungry." Ravenous, in fact.

"Me too. Smells great around here." Louise sniffed the air, heavy with garlic and basil.

"Y'all see anything that looks good?" Mallory pointed to a menu posted next to an open door.

"Trattoria," Mom read slowly.

Mallory spoke with the young woman standing at the counter and then turned to motion them in.

"My, isn't he efficient," Mom whispered.

Arms wide, Mallory shepherded them through the door. Amazing how quickly the man had hit it off with her family. They'd always acted distant with Jason, as if they didn't quite know what to do with him. Of course, usually he'd been glued to the TV, watching football or baseball.

The four of them were seated, completing a table for eight.

Two middle-aged couples pored over the menu printed on yellow paper. From their conversation, they sounded British.

Behind a low counter, men in white aprons cooked with noisy efficiency. Kitchen utensils shining in their hands, they chopped vegetables, tasted steaming soups, and slid heavy pans of bread from an open oven that cranked the heat up a notch in the small restaurant.

Mom unfolded her napkin and turned to Mallory. "So what do you do for a living?"

Amy reached for her water. Bless her mother for always getting right to the point.

Her mother's question seemed to faze Mallory a bit. "Ah, well now, my family has several businesses... including jewelry."

"What a coincidence! Us too!" Aunt Emily trilled.

"You bet." Louise shook her head. "Emily and me, we make jewelry." She flicked one of her silver earrings and the dangling humming bird quivered in response. "Sell it at the art fairs. We even took second prize at Italian Fest last summer."

"So Amy was telling me. Very impressive." Mallory took a closer look.

"When my husband died, well, I had to do something." Louise gave a matter-of-fact nod, and Amy's heart squeezed. Her mother had been devastated when Dad died unexpectedly. Amy had been on the verge of moving back home when Aunt Em stepped in. What a relief when Mom took up Aunt Em's passion for jewelry making. They were darned good at it too.

"I'm so sorry." Mallory's voice dropped. In that moment, he

wasn't a polished man from Savannah. No, he was a sympathetic family friend, who recognized the pain. She wanted to hug him.

"Yep, Emily took a course at the art center, and she taught me." Mom took a deep breath and looked to her sister. "Pays the bills and we have lot of fun, don't we, Em?"

Aunt Em nodded. "A grand time."

In the background a familiar song was playing. The words might be in Italian, but there was no mistaking "Strangers in the Night."

"Who is this singing?" Amy asked the waitress when she brought over their lunch.

Cocking her head to one side, the young girl listened. "Oh, Mark Masri. *Meraviglioso*, no? Very popular."

"Beautiful," she said, Aunt Em and Mom nodding.

But the haunting number sung with such emotion sent a chill through her. Right now, she felt comfortable with Mallory, but weren't they really strangers?

The song sounded a warning.

"So, tell me again," Mom said after they'd made short work of the soup and started on their pasta. "How did you two meet? This *chum* thing?"

Amy slogged into the explanation, dragging her pride right behind her. "Internet. Just looking, you know. And for some reason, I thought Mallory was a woman."

Louise turned to Mallory. "Did you think my daughter was a man? With a name like Amy?"

Mallory's blue eyes narrowed. "Ma'am, I must admit, I *am* a healthy American male."

"Ah, aren't you the one." Mom nodded at Amy. "You were in a jam and he offered to help you out."

"Right." Aunt Em got this dreamy look on her face. "After all, you couldn't let this beautiful honeymoon go to waste."

The word "honeymoon" slapped onto the middle of the table like a cold frittata. The two British couples fell silent.

"By Jove," one of the men hooted. "Are you two on your *honeymoon?*"

The word echoed through the restaurant. Heads craned. Amy's cheeks flamed.

"No. Absolutely not." Shoulders slumping, she could not look up.

Reaching under the table, Aunt Em squeezed her hand.

Just then the waiter dropped the check in front of Mallory, who promptly snapped it up. He'd been doing a lot of that, but Amy had made him promise that they would figure all of this out at the end.

The heat and all this honesty were too much. She struggled to her feet. The others followed her out the door in silence.

Making a quick turn, Mom stood in the bright sunshine, mouth falling open as she took in the scene. "Isn't that something?"

The dome of the Duomo rose above the other buildings, its pink and white stone sparkling in the mid-day sun. Before long, the four of them were inside the cool darkness of the ancient cathedral.

Mallory lagged behind, and after about twenty minutes, it became clear he wanted to move on. He pulled his phone from his pocket. "Why don't I meet you outside? I have some business calls to make."

"Not a problem." Amy watched him walk toward the exit, dreading the questions Louise was sure to ask.

Of course, Mallory probably had some of his own.

Chapter 15

Honeymoon. Good God. That explained a lot.

After talking to Miriam, Mallory grabbed a table at one of the cafes facing the Duomo.

This trip had taken some unexpected turns. He liked it. Hard to keep a straight face when Louise Shaw asked him about his work. A mother, she wanted to make sure he was employed.

Good for her. And good for him too. Not many men had the opportunity to meet a woman's family.

Settling back, he enjoyed the sun on his face. Even if he told Amy's family he was Mallory Thornton of Thornton Enterprises, they might not be impressed. Pretty damn refreshing.

Waving the waiter away, he kept an eye on the entrance to the cathedral. In the square in front of him, pigeons fluttered and pecked, hopping toward any crumb thrown by visitors. Travelers gathered at the small tables around him to people watch and consult maps. He leafed through a menu with pictures for those who didn't speak Italian. Not hungry, he tucked the menu back in the metal holder. Lunch had been filling in more ways than one. A lot to process.

After the last couple of days in very tight quarters, he felt he knew Amy Shaw better than he'd known his first wife. Not only was the Chicago teacher attractive, she was also practical. Thoughtful. Voluptuous. Sexy.

Lord, it was getting hot in this square.

Mallory edged under the umbrella shading the table. Amy was fun. He liked her and enjoyed being with her. Just that simple. But land sakes, was any woman ever simple?

As he sat in the outdoor cafe, he looked around. Over to one side sprawled an open-air market. What woman didn't like to shop? Satisfied with his plan for the afternoon, he settled in and made some more calls. Before too long, Louise appeared in the doorway of the Duomo, slipping her sunglasses into place, with Amy and Aunt Em trailing behind her.

On his feet in a second, he gave them a broad wave. The trio fell silent as Mallory approached. He'd bet five euros they'd been talking about him.

Mallory pointed to the left. "Think I spotted a market nearby. Would you ladies care to…"

Like a flock of geese, all three turned in unison.

The canopied booths in the market faced each other in long, ragged lines. Warmed by the sun, the pungent scent of leather rose from the wallets and coiled belts heaped on a table. Colorful scarves fluttered from another booth. The ladies had to touch everything and consult with each other. Amy's mother seemed the type who could talk to a tree and the tree would answer. Of course, all the vendors wanted to haggle. No problem with these ladies.

This open air bartering contrasted with the elegant Rodeo Drive in Beverly Hills or Michigan Avenue in Chicago, where Rhonda had dragged Mallory in their short time together. Quick to end her job at the bank, his bride had devoted herself to shopping after the wedding. She'd done a lot of plastic damage in a very short time.

"You really enjoy this, don't you?" Mallory commented as he drew closer to Amy.

Her green eyes sparkled. The sun brought out her freckles, and the midday heat caused her delicate skin to flush. "Doesn't everyone love a market?"

"Actually, I was referring to being with your family."

Amy shrugged. "Nothing unusual about it."

"Maybe for you." Rhonda hardly ever called her mother, or her older brother. One time when Rhonda's brother Jeff had called, she'd asked Mallory to tell him she wasn't home. Instead, Mallory had handed her the phone. His loving wife had been furious.

Chad had once told Mallory that if you wanted to see what a woman would look like in thirty years, just look at her mother. Mallory had not seen Rhonda's mother until the wedding. Myra Fairchuck had been a sad train wreck, wandering from one drink station to the next, calling everyone "hon."

Now Mallory regarded Louise with some interest. The lady was vibrant, interested in life, and in good physical shape. Her daughter took after her.

Amy looked back at her mother and aunt, who were debating which color scarf would suit Emily best. "They may be crazy, but they're all mine."

"You're very lucky."

"Well, you have family too."

Mallory shook his head. "Just my cousin, aunt, and my uncle."

"That's family."

"True," Mallory said shortly. The concern on Amy's face told him she understood. Felt good when he didn't have to hold up cue cards.

On a table up ahead was a display of sexy lingerie. After all, Italy prided itself as the land of *La Dolce Vida*. Mere wisps of lace, the bras and thongs sure weren't practical, but then good lingerie was meant to be appreciated, not functional.

At least, that was his theory.

Wearing a wistful expression, Amy reached out to touch a lacy black thong.

The middle-aged matron tending the table bolted to her feet. "No! No touch! Just to look." After wagging one finger in warning, the woman straightened the display with exaggerated care, as if the careless American had plundered her merchandise.

Amy stepped back. The longing in her face tugged at Mallory's heart in the strangest way.

Hooking the sheer black thong with one finger, he swung it toward the woman behind the table. "Ah, *signora*, we'll take this. In fact, three if you have them." He held up three fingers.

Amy gasped. Giving Amy a knowing look, the woman managed a small smile, as if to say that she had greatly misjudged her.

"Oh, these are not for me!" Amy's cheeks flamed and he choked back a laugh.

The shopkeeper got busy, wrapping the thongs in tissue and slipping them into a bright pink plastic bag. She was not about to lose a sale because of a squeamish American.

"Amy, every woman should have at least one black thong. Of course these are for you...unless of course Aunt Em or your mother..."

Amy held up one hand. "Oh, my gosh, no."

"Well, then. A gift."

"But not for me," she insisted. "Probably for a lady friend?"

Signing the receipt, Mallory shook his head slowly. "Would I be here if I had a lady friend? Do I seem like that type of man?"

"Your sister then."

"No sister."

"But what about Miriam?"

He had no idea what she was talking about.

Amy's expression brought it all back with a jolt.

"Of course. Miriam. Not quite her thing." His executive assistant leaned toward gray suits and blouses with high collars. He pushed the bag toward Amy. Pink bags weren't *his* thing. "Trust me, a little black thong should be a staple in every woman's closet."

"But not for Miriam?"

"Sadly, no. Not Miriam...or women who are like Miriam," he said pointedly.

"I see." Amy took the bag from his hands.

"Maybe you could help me choose something Miriam *would* like?" His assistant would be tickled if he brought her a gift.

Obviously, he'd struck a chord. A smile tilted Amy's lips.

"I'm sure Miriam would appreciate it." Every time he said Miriam's name, Amy softened a little more, her green eyes turning to summer limes. Scanning the tables, Amy took her time. Mallory followed behind, enjoying the way the sun caught the blonde streaks in Amy's hair, fighting the urge to touch one.

"You think she's not into..." Amy swept one hand over the tables of clearly erotic displays of lingerie.

"Oh, how I wish she were into black lace. It would probably help things." Mallory shook his head with what he hoped was convincing regret.

"Oh, dear." Amy paused.

"Not married." Dropping his voice, Mallory leaned closer. The scent of her coconut sunblock loosened every muscle in his body. All but one. "An unclaimed treasure, if you will."

Amy's face emptied. "How sad."

Mallory gave her a wry smile. "Very, but she needs to relax. Loosen up."

"Loosen up?" Amy straightened.

Time to poke the bear, as Chad would say. "Miriam's a little uptight. A lady with a schedule, not that a schedule is a bad thing. After all, she does have responsibilities." Mallory circled close enough to inhale that sunblock again and detect the spicy orange scent Amy spritzed on herself in the morning. Felt strange, getting to know her personal habits. So intimate.

Amy searched his face before her eyes fell. "Scheduled, huh?"

"Organization can be a good thing sometimes." But it was too late. Amy's face fell. He felt like a heel. Sometimes you could poke the bear a little too hard and break the skin.

Not with Amy. Not from him.

They'd reached a table piled high with linens of crisp white, pale pink or yellow. A white cloth hung overhead with lacy something-or-other joining squares of fabric—the kind of linen his grandmother once brought out for a holiday dinner.

"What about one of these?" Amy asked. "Tablecloths are always good."

He nodded. "Miriam might like these."

Hand sorting the piles efficiently, Amy eventually pulled out a pale lemon folded square. "What about this?"

"You know, I think she might prefer white." White seemed like a sensible choice. And Miriam was certainly sensible.

"Your sister must be very traditional." Amy laid the yellow linen aside and snagged a white replacement. "Done deal?"

"Done deal," Mallory echoed, handing the tablecloth to a waiting saleswoman just as Louise and Emily strolled toward them, heads together and bags hanging from their arms.

"Want to share our shopping with your family?" Mallory asked, watching her smile straighten into a leaden line. "Get their opinion?"

"There are some things I don't share with my family." When the woman handed her a plain white bag, Amy quickly stashed the pink plastic inside. Mallory swallowed a laugh.

After Louise and Emily caught up, the four of them spent the rest of the afternoon wandering from shop to shop while Mallory observed. Their family dynamics fascinated him.

Being an only child in the Thornton line had been a responsibility. Even as a child, Mallory had understood that. From the start, his father was far more interested in training than in education. Rules. That's all Mallory remembered. Teachers commented that he was bright, but he lacked focus. ADD wasn't on the scene yet. His mother ended up running interference for him with his father, which put them at odds. That didn't make anyone happy.

If he was ever lucky enough to have a son, Mallory would make sure his son ran and played like the other guys.

By five o'clock, the women's attention had turned from their formidable collection of bags to dinner. A quick call to Caitlin revealed she and Kurt were tied up.

"Caitlin's in love," Louise said in an undertone to Mallory while Amy said goodbye and pocketed the phone. "I'm hoping for another wedding."

"Louise," Aunt Em prodded gently, eyes darting to Amy.

"Sorry. A wedding," Louise corrected herself, and Amy sighed.

There it was again. Sure he had questions, but he wanted Amy to answer them. Maybe he would have a chance to learn more during dinner. They set up a tentative time and decided to meet at the restaurant.

Amy fell silent after her mother and aunt went on their way. "Tired?" he asked as they ambled toward the hotel.

Pushing her hair behind one shell-like ear, Amy caught a strand and bit down on it. "Maybe we need some alone time."

"The two of us? I agree." Funny, he felt a little disappointed. He'd enjoyed time with Louise and Emily.

"No, I meant each of us might need some time alone."

Hell's bells. What was this? They were approaching the hotel, and he turned to face her. He thought the day had gone pretty damn well. "Is this like a trial separation?" Irritation razored Mallory's words.

They reached the front entrance. The doorman snapped to attention, holding the glass door wide. Amy hesitated. Then she stepped through, chin down.

Now she'd hurt his feelings. Inside the hotel lobby, Amy glanced up at Mallory. He'd been such a good guy, accepting her family and everything. The pink bag was crunched in her backpack. She couldn't even go there. Her black thongs were all at home. Shopping for one with a man? First time for everything. Sometimes this week felt totally out of control. She wanted to talk to her family alone. Explanations were in order. "Just for this evening, okay?"

"Sure. Fine."

But it wasn't. Mallory's face had hardened into disappointed ridges. Reaching out, she tugged his hand. "Just tonight, okay?"

A corner of his mouth tweaked up. "Fine. But just for tonight."

Felt like they'd just agreed on something, but she wasn't sure exactly what that something might be.

Chapter 16

Rolling over with a yawn, Mallory stretched. The sheets smelled so damn good. But different. He pried his eyes open and rolled toward the other bed. The morning light caressed Amy's curves. Damn.

What a beauty. Peachy skin and light freckles. Golden curls tossed against the pillow and lips slightly open. His body registered an immediate response. Good God, his hands tingled as he imagined skimming that soft skin. A healthy imagination took him to areas he hadn't seen...yet.

Falling flat on his back, he shoved his hands behind his head and studied the ceiling. The night before had been deadly dull. Even a call to Chad failed to lift his mood. His cousin had teased him unmercifully, and he'd said very little. Finally Chad asked him why he'd called. Downright testy. Short conversation.

After an uneventful dinner in some cafe, he'd wandered back over the bridge toward the hotel. At the highest point, a man and woman had drawn a small crowd. While the guy strummed a beat-up guitar, they sang what sounded like a French love song, a hat at their feet.

He wanted Amy there with him. After tossing some bills in the hat, he took off. A lot to think about as he strolled back to the hotel.

Was he, Mallory Thornton, actually missing someone? When Rhonda moved out, taking her heavy perfumes and reality TV shows with her, he was so damned relieved. Stretching out on the leather sofa in the TV room, he'd snapped on a game and cracked open a beer. Relaxed and enjoyed his newfound freedom.

One evening without his travel chum, and he was bored out of his skull. Was it the clean scent of her sunblock or her cute giggle?

Or was it the fact she was part of a family he liked very much?

By the time Mallory had returned to the hotel room, Amy was tucked in her twin bed like some nun, a sheet pulled up to her chin. Apparently she liked the heavy silk drapes open. Moonlight fell across the bed in thick, creamy waves.

Amy had looked luminous—like a woman in a Rossetti painting. His mother had made him take Art Appreciation in prep school. Finally it paid off. Yes sir, Amy was full-on Rossetti. Generous lips. Heavy eyes and all that long, wavy hair. And yet, she had such innocence about her. Good God, she'd blushed scarlet when he'd teased her about the thong. Almost made him feel guilty.

Almost, but not quite.

He sure wasn't a good judge of women. Rhonda was proof of that. But he'd become an excellent judge of families. So far, Amy's folks ranked high on his list. Could a woman coming from that family be deceitful? He doubted it.

Restless and lonely, he'd had trouble falling asleep with a beautiful woman within his reach but so far away.

Amy gave a deep heartfelt sigh as she rolled toward him, the sheet slipping below the tank top she wore at night. The top didn't cover much.

He'd always been a believer that suggestion was a bigger turn-on than full nudity. He studied her curves and imagined.

Good God, enough.

Careful not to wake Amy, he threw back the covers and padded through the thick green carpet toward the bathroom. As he showered, Mallory mentally reviewed the calendar. Land sakes, the week was wasting away. It was Wednesday and high time to advance his strategy.

Did he have a plan?

Stay with Amy. All week.

The stupid bet began to make sense. Hadn't it brought her to him? He was starting to feel grateful for Chad's nonsense.

Minutes later, he pulled on some clothes and quietly scribbled a note. As he closed the door to their room, she began to rustle in her bed, making all kinds of luscious stretches. He had to get out of there.

When Amy showed up in the cozy breakfast room of the hotel, Mallory was savoring his Italian coffee. Wearing a soft peach T-shirt and a dark green mini skirt with a matching sweatshirt knotted around her waist, Amy glowed. The saffron walls complemented her coloring. Blondish curls slipped from the pony tail that bounced when she walked.

Full-on Miss Sandusky. *Damn.*

He sprang to his feet. "My, oh, my. Don't you just look like a

Georgia peach this morning."

Flashing a shy smile, Amy slid into the chair opposite him. "When I was a little girl, my mother would always dress me in peach—her favorite color, not mine. Now I like it. Go figure." A dainty lift of one shoulder and she reached for the coffee pot.

Mallory chuckled. "Why does that not surprise me that you gave Louise a hard time about your clothes?"

"So it shows, huh?"

"A bit." He leaned toward her, hoping to capture that citrus scent that drove him crazy. "How was last evening?"

"My family missed you." A note of disbelief echoed in Amy's voice.

"No kidding?" Mallory felt positively tickled.

"Sorry if I offended you by suggesting time alone." She picked at a croissant. "I just thought it might be a good idea. Stupid really."

"The teacher in you? Getting things organized."

Amy grimaced before she took her first sip of coffee. "Maybe. I'm still getting over the shock of seeing them all here. But at least, the, ah, situation gave them an excuse to make this trip. Mom and Aunt Em have booked a five-day stay here in Florence. Caitlin and Kurt are moving on to Venice." She hesitated, her gaze flashing to his.

"Fine with me," Mallory assured her. So far Caitlin and Kurt had been pretty absorbed with each other. "So, today the Uffizi is the first stop?"

"Gosh, I've read about that museum for so long. Can't wait to see *The Birth of Venus*," she murmured, face brightening as if she were already in front of the masterpiece. Her excitement was contagious.

Anticipation revved through his veins. "Botticelli."

"You know it?"

"Sure. Art class. All I can remember about that painting, if I have it right, is really long hair, broken by the strategic placement of Venus' hand." Erotic as hell. Amy probably had no idea she'd strongly resembled the masterpiece as she rose from the waters in Monterosso.

"Sounds wonderful. Can't wait."

But a melancholy note in her voice snapped him to attention. Damn, what had he said now? Amy's eyes were filling while she played with the packets of sugar. "You probably have questions after my family's comments yesterday."

"A few, yes, but when you're ready."

"Jason was more than a friend, okay? Jason was…my fiancé. Our wedding was called off at the last minute. There were some, ah, complications."

"I'm so sorry." He appreciated the honesty.

Her blush deepened. "The truth is, he preferred a physical education teacher over me, I guess. Caught them together in the locker room shower. I just didn't want to give up this…honeymoon." She could hardly get the last word out.

A waitress arrived.

"Nothing for me, thank you. I'm not hungry," Amy told her.

"I'm also fine, thank you, ma'am."

The waitress left.

Mallory considered what to say while Amy continued to shred a croissant. "Amy, the man's not worth a second of regret."

"I know it." Tears ran down her cheeks.

He handed her a napkin.

"Maybe it was awful to involve you in my mistake."

Good God, she was killing him. Her story wasn't any more pitiful than his own.

"We both signed up on that site, Amy. For what it's worth, I can tell you it's better to call the wedding off now than regret it later."

Amy's gaze latched onto his. "Are you are talking about your short marriage? Bad experience, huh?"

His attempt at a laugh came out a bark. "Trust me, my marriage was more than a bad experience. More like being flayed alive."

"I'm so sorry, Mallory." The huskiness of her voice stroked every sensitive cord in his body.

"A mistake from the very beginning." His coffee had turned lukewarm and he set the cup down.

This would be a good chance to open up. He could come clean. Tell her about the bet and the car. He opened his mouth, but nothing came out. What would she think? He'd feel like a total fool, and he snapped his mouth shut just as she glanced up.

Where this was headed, a confession might ruin everything. He wasn't going to risk it.

"What about your parents' marriage?" Amy heaped what was left of her croissant with orange marmalade and dug in as if she hadn't eaten in days.

"Although my father could be inconsiderate, my mother made up for it." Images of happier times flooded his mind. "I never realized it could be so hard. Marriage that is."

A frown puckered her forehead. "Maybe good marriages just make it look easy. My mother really misses my dad. They were good friends."

Amy might be the kind of woman who'd be a great friend. The thought was novel and unsettling. He checked his watch. "Maybe we should move along. You don't want to miss your family."

"We're meeting them after the Uffizi at the statue of David. Since they're staying in Florence after we leave, they wanted to devote an entire day to the museum."

Mallory left any regrets about his hesitation at the table. He could probably look all over hell and half of Georgia and not find a woman like Amy. He wasn't about to spoil it.

Sprinting down the narrow streets in the freshness of the morning, Amy felt her spirits lift. Telling the truth had brought relief. Birds twittered overhead, and shopkeepers hosed the sidewalks in front of their storefronts.

This solo honeymoon—well, except for Mallory and her family—she'd finally come to terms with it.

Mallory took her hand. Picking up the pace, she laced her fingers through his.

When they finally found the Uffizi, a line of restless tourists stretched down the long portico and into the street. They joined the group. The cool morning air held an early September dampness that hinted at fall. Unknotting her green sweatshirt from around her waist, she slipped her arms into the sleeves with Mallory's help.

"You're very well trained. You know that?" she kidded him.

"Yes, ma'am," he teased, thickening his southern accent. "My dear mother sure did, ma'am." His hands rested on her shoulders.

The conversation ahead of them became heated, and the German father made a chopping motion with his hands. "*Kaput!*" he exclaimed while his wife nodded in stolid agreement. Their two teenage sons looked chastened.

"*Kaput.*" Mallory's lips were warm against her ear. "I do declare. Sounds like my ill-fated marriage."

His lips tickled and she smiled. "My relationship too. *Kaput.* Thank goodness."

Now, when had her feelings about that canceled wedding changed to relief? Ear still tingling, she tried to squelch the heat shimmering through her body. But why? One deep breath and she released her longing for Mallory in delicious waves that would lead who knew where.

As the crowded packed closer, Amy wound up leaning against Mallory. He looped one arm around her waist. The warmth pulsing in her veins circled her stomach and dipped lower. The line moved forward, and his arm dropped.

But it had felt good. Way too good.

Finally they reached the counter, got their tickets, and dropped off Amy's backpack in the checkroom. Mallory grabbed a map, and they took the wide stone steps to the wide gallery above. Upstairs, the sun shone brightly through leaded glass windows onto an assortment of marble statues. Various viewing rooms led off of the gallery. Their map was carefully marked by time period.

Amy stared at the diagram. "Guess we should do this historically."

"Or we could just go for the good stuff first." Mallory's blue eyes narrowed with a challenge.

Grabbing his hand, she tugged him into the nearest room.

As they wandered through gallery after gallery, Amy became distracted by the brush of Mallory's body, the scent of his aftershave, the eyes that focused totally on her when he talked about a painting. Longing rippled through her body in rich waves.

How amazing. Here she stood, surrounded by breathtaking art, and all she could think about was Mallory's impossibly thick mane of dark hair. How would it feel in her hands? Heavy and substantial, the type that clung to your fingers when she cupped his head?

Anticipation left her trembling.

Finally, they reached *The Birth of Venus*. "Here we go." Mallory pulled up short in front of the masterpiece. "My, oh, my. Botticelli."

"So you really know this artist's work?" Pretty impressive.

Mallory threw her an *aw shucks* look. "Yes, ma'am. Took that art class to please my mother."

"I think I would have liked your mother." His pinched look made her feel terrible. "Sorry, Mallory."

"Not a problem."

But it was. After all, he didn't have much family. Shoulder to shoulder, they viewed the painting. How could one woman look so innocent and so seductive at the same time? Venus balanced on the open shell, reddish blonde hair spilling to her feet, delicate hands covering key areas of her body.

Almost nude but not quite. Amy's breath caught in her throat. Her own body tingling, she dug her camera out of her pocket.

The guard stationed in the corner jerked toward her at the same time that Mallory grabbed her hand. "Sorry," he said to the guard, who fell back.

"Oh, of course. What was I thinking?"

"Not a problem." Mallory handed the camera to her. "If everyone took pictures, the paintings might be damaged."

"I just wanted something to remember this by," she explained in a shaky voice. "The painting, I mean."

"Hmm, yes. Beautiful." But Mallory's eyes were on her, not the painting.

"All that hair." Pulling her gaze back to Venus, she wondered how long it took to grow hair that touched the floor.

"Flowing over her body," he whispered.

"And her delicate hands…"

"Unfortunate but necessary placement."

"She's, well, beautiful." Stuttering, she dropped her eyes. "I mean, the painting. The painting is beautiful."

"So you…like it?"

She swallowed. "Oh, yes."

Crazy, but the conversation sure felt like foreplay, only better.

A large group of Chinese tourists entered the gallery, their guide launching into commentary. Mallory turned to leave, and Amy stumbled after him, reaching for his hand.

In a nearby section, they discovered the reclining Venus. "More strategic placement of the hands," she murmured as they stood before the painting, looking at the work with fresh eyes.

Would she have felt this way if she were here with Jason? Somehow, she doubted it.

They exited from the last room in the long corridor. "We could spend all day here, but we probably should leave to meet my family." She took out her phone and checked the time.

"David, it is," Mallory said, looking around. "Staircase this way."

Together they made their way from the Uffizi to the Academy Gallery, which housed the statue of David.

"Amy!" Louise bustled toward them when they entered the long hall. At the end, David rose majestically, surrounded by gaping tourists. Mom looked from Mallory to Amy with open curiosity. "Where've you been? You're missing it, honey."

"The Uffizi. You'll love it," she told her mother.

"Hi, chickadee." Her aunt hugged her and then put one cool hand on her forehead, like she was ten. "You okay? Look a little feverish."

Unzipping her sweatshirt, she slipped it from her shoulders. "I'm fine. Temperature in these buildings keeps changing."

"Isn't he impressive?" her mother gazed at the seventeen foot sculpture with awe.

Mallory looked up. "Nothing to criticize here."

All parts of David were huge.

Caitlin and Kurt arrived a few minutes later. "We decided to sleep in. After all, we are on vacation."

Right. People always flew across the ocean to hole up in their room.

But maybe Caitlin had a point.

Maybe a trip shouldn't be all about museums.

Chapter 17

After the museums, they wandered about the city and settled into a cozy trattoria for lunch. Mallory loved watching the family dynamics, including Amy's attempts to deflect any personal questions he might ask.

Damn shame, because Louise seemed to be eager to tell all.

After lunch, it was off for more shopping. Mallory and Kurt trailed behind and became the "beasts of burden," as Mallory put it. Amy made a point of hanging onto her own bags, even though he'd offered to carry them. She was not one to trust anyone, Mallory decided—and maybe with reason. He wanted to punch out Jason.

Before they all went their separate ways, they agreed to meet for dinner. No comment was made about "time alone." Hot damn. Not wanting to wander around the city looking for a suitable restaurant, he'd done a little research earlier and asked questions of shopkeepers while the ladies were busy at the counters.

"La Nandina has good reviews," he suggested.

"Sounds dandy." Louise checked her family circle for agreement.

"Fabulous." Caitlin gave Mallory a sideways glance. "You are definitely a man who knows his way around."

"Let's wait until after we taste the food." Mallory hoped the restaurant was all the man in the pottery shop had promised.

Amy had been so quiet. More than once, he'd looked up to find those gold-flecked green eyes on him, warm and appraising. When he smiled, she looked away. Would be a dead giveaway at a poker table.

With all their eccentricities, Amy's family was growing on him. As an only child, he'd missed out on the teasing between siblings. Like Amy and Caitlin, Louise and Emily engaged in sisterly sparring. Lots of inside jokes, half-finished sentences. Fascinating.

Is this what it might be like if he had a family of his own? Would this be possible instead of the stiff formality of his own upbringing? Might have been different if he'd had siblings. His mother had been grateful when Mallory came along. That's just how she put it.

Owen Thornton had not been at all happy with the small size of his family. Not enough potential for the Thornton Dynasty. In a lot of ways, Mallory was never enough.

Looking at the Shaw group, he'd choose this easy openness anytime. No expectations. No disappointments—at least that he could see.

And Amy? His stomach clenched every time she gave him one of her mysterious smiles.

"You're awfully quiet," she said as they headed back to the hotel.

"A lot to think about."

"Those paintings, huh?" Her smile tilted with mischief.

He took her hand. "Reality is always better, don't you think?"

Nipping her lower lip between her teeth, she nodded.

"Something you can actually see and touch."

Her shiver reverberated to the tips of her fingers. He tightened his grip.

Getting dressed for dinner wasn't as uncomfortable as it had been in Rapallo. Sure, they traded places, but it worked. That is, until she came out of the bathroom in the slinky, sea green gown from Monterosso. Then all bets were off.

"You look beautiful...gorgeous." Words failed him. That didn't happen often.

"Thank you." She ran one hand over the skirt that accented her curves.

The dipping neckline and clingy skirt made him want to loosen his tie. He'd actually dressed for this dinner, hoping to make a good impression.

Since when had that mattered?

"Shall we?" He stepped to the door. They had to get out of this bedroom.

On their way to the restaurant, they picked up Louise and Aunt Em and then continued on. "We've been waiting for you." Caitlin teased as they met at the front door of La Nandina. "Great dress, Amy."

"Something new," Amy murmured.

Catching sight of a black shadow across her hips under the fabric, Mallory's imagination ran wild.

The thong? Damn, this was torture.

"We're not that late, Caitlin, are we?" Louise reached up to fluff her hair.

"On vacation, there's no such thing as being late." Kurt opened the door.

"My man, I do agree." Mallory ushered the ladies inside. Low lights glowed in the center of circular tables. The spicy scent of tomato sauce and grilled vegetables hung heavy in the air. From the comfortable look of the diners, the shopkeeper who'd recommended La Nandina had been right on target. Looked like a local haunt.

"When I get back to the room tonight, I have to write out my postcards," Louise said after they ordered. She showed no signs of being tired after tromping all over Florence.

Amy's mother was amazing, but then she couldn't be that old. He really missed his mother. Anne Thornton might have been just this uninhibited if she'd married another man. Much to his father's disgust, his wife had been happy with quiet pursuits, like gardening. Owen Thornton preferred his wife to be at the club, positioned as a recognized society woman, playing golf and tennis. His mother had never been interested in that role.

"You'll be home before the postcards, Mom," Amy pointed out.

"The boys'll get the point." Louise took another sip of her wine. "What's the use of going away if you don't remind people that you've been gone?"

"Boys?" Sometimes it was hard keeping up with this group. Mallory loved it.

"Mom has three male friends…escorts, really—Ralph, Wally and Fred," Amy explained with an impish grin.

Louise gave her daughter a small nudge, her eyes flashing with mischief. "You make it sound like I'm some kind of wild woman." She turned to Mallory. "I square dance with Ralph, play bridge with Wally, and go to the movies with Fred. Can you beat that? Can't get a man who's got everything, I guess."

"Is that the secret?" Would Amy be a card like Louise when she got older? Probably. This unasked-for review of her family was priceless. By rushing to her rescue, Amy's family had given Mallory a rare opportunity.

"What about you two?" Mom's eyes brightened with curiosity. "What's on tap for you tomorrow?"

Amy's shoulders squeezed together. "Venice."

"Venice," Louise breathed. "My, how grand."

"We're going to San Gimignano tomorrow," Aunt Emily offered.

"Beautiful hill town. Fabulous towers." Mallory began to describe the town when he felt Amy's eyes on him. Too late, he remembered he was Mallory Schuster, a man of limited means. "Or so I've heard."

"Next time, I'm going to apply for a travel chum," Louise clucked. "This has worked out just great for you."

Amy played with her silver necklace. "Nothing's really *worked out*, Mom."

But only because they hadn't had a chance. This family time had been great but a bit of an interruption. Twirling his wine glass in his fingers, Mallory planned on regaining ground. Every time he looked at her, he liked the view more. Maybe it was that dress and the way it clung to her luscious curves. Maybe it was the glint of the silver earrings against her hair, or the pink tongue that flicked out to wet her lips.

Every time he looked at her tonight, Mallory lost his train of thought.

His body didn't.

In the background, music played. Didn't understand a word but no mistaking "O Sole Mio"—such emotion. He turned to Amy. "Isn't this the same guy our waitress mentioned at the trattoria?"

She listened, her lips curving upward. "Definitely. Mark Masri, wasn't it?"

"Talk about throwing your whole heart into it."

Louise pulled out a little notebook and jotted down the name. He remembered his own grandmother always having a notebook with her.

"Honey, those earrings look great on you," Louise commented as they continued with dinner.

Amy touched one of the beaten silver ovals. "Made by the best."

He leaned closer. The style was simple but elegant and matched the pendant suspended between Amy's breasts. "Lovely."

Amy's eyes widened, following his gaze to her cleavage.

"And where are these sold?" Mallory adopted his professional tone.

Louise waved a hand. "Oh, art fairs, flea markets."

Sure sounded like a haphazard distribution plan. "Why not market them in one of the larger retailers?"

Louise stared at him blankly. "I wouldn't know how."

"Mom, we've talked about it." But even Amy sounded perplexed.

"I have a small display of Mom's and Aunt Em's jewelry in my shop," Caitlin offered.

"Tell me a little bit about your shirt shop." His mind started spinning.

"T-shirts." Caitlin motioned toward Amy. "All those cute shirts my sister wears."

"Ah, yes. *Read it*," Mallory mused, remembering his first encounter with Amy when he couldn't keep his eyes off the quaint saying stretched across her chest.

So both Amy's mother and sister were involved in small, female-owned businesses. The board's suggestion came back to him. This trip could accomplish more than one goal. Mallory settled back. His stomach churned while his earlier bet locked horns with the sweet, sexy woman next to him.

At some point, he had to resolve this situation.

"What about you two?" Amy asked Caitlin and Kurt as they sat with their coffee after dinner. "You stay here too?"

"Headed to Venice but don't worry. We won't be dogging your trail. I'd copied your itinerary before, you know…" Caitlin glanced toward Mallory and then dropped her eyes.

Mallory might have Amy all to himself in Venice. Brought a rush of heat. He wanted to make the most of every minute. Time seemed too short.

Amy and Mallory walked Louise and Aunt Emily back to their hotel. The air felt surprisingly soft for fall. Kurt and Caitlin had gone their way. This evening had been pretty near perfect. Amy felt decidedly sexy in her new dress. Would she ever wear it again? It might hang in her closet next to her wedding gown.

But for tonight, she wore the dress like hope.

"Ask the man at the desk if you have any questions. Don't go out after dark." Amy began to list her safety rules for her mother and aunt as they said good night. She felt more than a little nervous at the thought of the two of them on their own in Florence.

Mom waved her concerns away. "Don't you worry, honey. Em and me, we'll be fine."

"I'll take care of things, dear." Linking arms with Mom, Aunt Em winked at Amy.

"Let me give you my card." Mallory reached inside his jacket. Then he stopped, a curious expression on his face. "But I don't seem to have any. Louise, would you by any chance happen to have a piece of paper?"

Mom lived for these moments. In seconds, she'd produced her tiny blue spiral notebook along with a pen.

Mallory scratched something on one page and handed the notebook back to Mom. "If y'all have any questions, any concerns, I want you to call me. Hear now?"

"Aren't you a sweetie?" Louise tucked the notebook back in her purse with a sly smile. "Really, Mallory, we wouldn't think of bothering you two."

Sometimes Amy wanted to strangle her mother.

"Most of our time will be taken up with the bus trips we have lined up," Aunt Em supplied.

"In any case, ladies, call me at this number if the slightest question arises." Mallory's voice held a decisive edge. Amy hadn't heard this tone, except when he asked for the car keys. "Any time, day or night."

Both women nodded. The air cleared, and Amy kissed them both on the cheek. Not the trip she'd planned but this family time had been special. Mallory and Amy saw that the two were safely inside before continuing on to their own hotel.

"What characters," Amy murmured.

"Charming." Mallory fell into step next to her. "You're lucky."

When had things changed with Mallory? She'd tried to put the stranger from Savannah in a box when she first realized he was her travel chum. The kiss when they arrived in Rapallo had taken her by surprise. Saving her life in the Rapallo restaurant? A real game changer. He'd been so sweet with her family today. That's when she'd felt the real tug on her heart.

He knew her and liked her.

And they had so little time left.

Chapter 18

The streets of Florence held the hush of evening when Amy and Mallory pushed on to their own hotel. Street lamps cast deep shadows over her travel chum's features, and an unwelcome shiver passed through her. Hard to read Mallory in broad daylight. Night shadows? Impossible. When Amy stumbled, he steadied her. "Everything okay?"

"Perfect." She wanted to sink into his arms. They both hesitated and then pushed on to the Ponte Vecchio. A brisk night breeze was blocked by the shops now shuttered along the bridge. The cool blast of air when they reached the other end made Amy wish she'd brought a shawl.

"You're freezing." Slipping out of his jacket, Mallory draped it around her shoulders. The soft wool smelled like him, and she cuddled into it. When she glanced up, his eyes were liquid navy pools. "All better?"

She nodded, and Mallory pulled her closer. "Thanks for sharing your family with me."

"Not what you expected when you signed on...my relatives, I mean," she stuttered. "I didn't need to be, well, rescued."

His laugh rumbled deep in his chest. "Most certainly not. But it's been fun."

"At least I didn't choke today. Or fall into the water."

"Saints be praised and amen."

She started to laugh but stopped when Mallory bent closer, his body heat welcoming her. "Amy Shaw," he whispered, tracing her cheek with one finger. "Who would have thought?"

"Thought what?"

"Just having a better time than I expected." His hand traveled to the back of her neck.

"You're not the only one." She lifted her face.

The first kiss barely brushed her lips. "More, please."

Mallory's hands cupped her face, like she was one of the delicate Lladro figurines they'd seen that day. With a strangled groan, he rained slow kisses on her face until she was in full-out tremble. Grasping his shoulders, she pulled him to her with a kiss, lips open and searching while he tasted.

"Yum. You still taste like merlot."

"Are you partial to red wine?"

"Think I'm partial to you."

"Take a sip," Mallory urged, voice ragged.

Amy pressed into him with a sigh.

A couple passed them on the street, and Mallory drew back after a kiss that could have gone on forever and still been too short. "I do believe we might be making a spectacle of ourselves, wanton woman from Chicago."

"Wanton?" She loved the round, ripe sound.

They walked on, fingers laced and her body humming. At the hotel, the doorman greeted them. Lighting dimmed, the lobby seemed more intimate than in the daytime. Their footsteps echoed on the marble floor. The registrar at the desk offered a polite nod. Italians were so discreet. The man studied a computer screen, as if he didn't notice their rush toward the bank of elevators.

Her breath was coming in tight gasps when the elevator arrived with a soft ping. "How chummy do you think this could get?" Mallory asked with a guarded smile as the doors closed behind them.

"Very."

His eyes warmed. "Damn, you're beautiful, Amy."

On Mallory's lips, her name sounded beautiful.

And wanton. That too.

They fell into a heated kiss, her hands raking into his hair. Who noticed when his jacket slipped from her shoulders? Hands on her hips, he snugged her to his body. His arousal felt so good. Her breasts sprang to life.

The elevator stopped, and the doors slid open. They broke apart, and Amy took a deep breath. Scooping up his jacket and taking her hand, Mallory led her down the quiet hall. Anticipation spiraled inside until she felt like a helium balloon on parade day. Once inside their room, he closed the door and turned to her, a question darkening his eyes.

"Yes," she whispered.

"Thank God." Groaning, he pressed her against the door with a slow, certain kiss. Amy shivered as his lips traveled to the hollow of her neck, threatening to turn her inside out. Her whole body throbbed *now*. "Oh, Mallory."

But the man had fallen into his southern mode.

He explored her body with leisurely appreciation. A little stroking here, some cupping there. Her body curved easily into his fingers, and her breathing tightened to gasps. The light pinching nearly sent her over the edge.

Sure, red flags kept flipping up, caution signs that she mowed down with a fierce passion, like one of those Olympic skiers on a slalom run. *Be a babe* echoed through her body as she careened down a slope of snowballing desire.

But a snowball would melt in this heat. Caution jerked her to a halt. "Just one thing. This week and nothing more." Maybe she was just reminding herself.

"Sure. Whatever." His hands got busy with her zipper.

She caught his chin in one hand. "I mean it, Mallory. No waiting for calls or texts. None of that."

A woman setting her boundaries. McKenna and Vanessa would be proud.

Did he look hurt? Must be her imagination.

"If that's what you want. Now, if we could get back to business." Thighs aligned, he backed her toward the closest bed.

As Amy melted, he hardened.

"Didn't...didn't mean to insult you," she managed, panting. She was panting, for Pete's sake.

"Look, I like you, Amy." He stopped.

"Like me?" Was this middle school?

"No, *really* like you. Damnation, I am not good at this." His frustration touched her heart, but the delay was killing the mood.

"Later." Yanking him close, she got him back on track.

The rim of the bed hit the back of her calves. She only wanted to set limits, protect herself. So hard to think with his lips roving over everything that wasn't covered and a couple of things that were.

When Mallory nudged her onto the bed, she kicked off her strappy aqua sandals and curled up on the green coverlet.

"If you were a cat now, darlin', you'd be purring."

"Can't you hear me?" Her heartbeat throbbed in her ears. Grabbing the hem of her dress, she pulled it up, but the zipper snagged her hair.

"Let me help before you scratch that beautiful skin…why, Amy." His eyes trailed from her filmy black bra to her clamped knees. He lifted a brow. "The thong?"

Thighs parting, she gave him a better look.

He tore at his tie. "Damn. What a gift."

"Time to unwrap it." She wiggled her fingers.

"Now, let's take our time."

"Now, let's not be so southern."

"Impatient, are we?" Balancing on the edge of the bed, he skimmed one hand from her shoulder to hip. Felt like he was unzipping her skin.

She sighed. "I'm beginning to like slow."

"If we're not careful, we'll both wind up on the floor." He nudged her over gently.

"Feels like I'm at camp on this tiny bed."

"I'm quite sure there are no scout medals for what we are about to do."

"Too bad. I'd want to earn them all."

"Over achiever."

First time that comment didn't sound like an insult.

Mallory opened the front clasp of her bra and whisked the straps down her arms.

"Good lord." His eyes burned.

She began to pull the pedant over her head, but his hand stopped her. "Trust me, it's lovely right where it is."

"Not in the way?"

"Never." He traced the inner curve of each breast. "Hot. Definitely hot."

That look would keep her warm on cold Chicago nights when he was a one-week memory.

Mallory fumbled with his shirt buttons, but he was taking so long. "One of us is wearing too many clothes, and it isn't me." One good yank, and she'd ripped the oxford cloth shirt open, buttons scattering.

"Hope the hotel in Venice has a tailor." Laughing, Mallory kicked off his slacks. Briefs came next. "Lordy, you *are* wanton."

"This is just the beginning." Amy settled back with a sigh.

"You've got that right." As Mallory aligned himself next to her, his need jutted against the softness of her stomach.

"You didn't tell me you resembled David." Her hands moved to the firm softness throbbing against her.

"Biggest compliment I've ever heard." He moaned, flicking his thumbs across the tips of her breasts. "I've been dying to do this all day."

"While we viewed those gorgeous paintings?"

"Nothing like good art to make a guy horny."

"Did you need them for inspiration?"

"Not with you. I have my hands full." And he proved it.

Her body's rush of liquid warmth tightened her hold, and he groaned.

Then she stopped.

"What?" His hands stilled.

Amy moved to cover her breasts. "Come on, I'm a lot bigger than the women in the paintings."

"Don't know what you're talking about." Mallory circled one of her wrists with one thumb and forefinger, forming an oval. "Look at how delicate you are."

"Delicate?" Delicate and wanton.

Could this night get any better?

Mallory cupped her cheek. "Trust me. You are special."

No, definitely not.

From somewhere, he produced a condom.

"You came prepared?" She should be relieved, not suspicious.

"Vintage supply."

He fit so well between her thighs, and she was beyond ready. With one sure stroke, he was inside. She gasped.

"You all right, darlin'?" All movement stopped.

"More than all right." Her legs wrapped around him.

The movements? Rugged and so right.

The feelings?

New. Had she ever felt like this before?

The answer terrified her.

Chapter 19

The breeze from the fields along the highway rolled over Amy in deep, fragrant waves. Wheat? Weeds? Didn't matter. Sleep deprivation had never felt this good. Sure, she'd had a boyfriend in college and then Jason. Nothing had prepared her for Mallory Schuster. But she was overthinking again. Giving a little stretch, she opened her car window wider.

For these few days, she was a babe.

No remorse. No cautious over-thinking.

Weird, but the appearance of her family had made things better, like some crazy aphrodisiac.

Mom and Aunt Em were back in Florence. Caitlin and Kurt were out on the road, also headed for Venice. Next to her, Mallory wore a sleepy smile. Silence stretched between them, comfortable and shared. Morning sunlight brightened the landscape and reflected off the hood of the car. Overnight, her life had become dazzling.

Every incredibly hot moment was imprinted on Amy's mind for snowy days when she worked on her lesson plan for *The Great Gatsby*. Every kiss, caress and groan would tide her over on those days when night fell before she made it to the parking lot.

"Tired?" Mallory asked.

"We didn't sleep much last night, in case you didn't notice."

"How could I not?" Rubbing a quick hand over his eyes, he yawned.

Amy smiled, hating the tentacles of caution that groped for her. Even her heart beat a cautionary tale. She was ignoring them.

Reaching into her backpack, she pulled out what was left of a bar of dark chocolate from Florence. The slightly bitter chocolate melted on her tongue. "Want some?"

"Oh, yes, ma'am, I sure do. But chocolate's not what I have in mind." Mallory's eyes met hers over the top of his aviator sunglasses.

The wedge of chocolate shot down Amy's throat. "Attention to the road, please."

Smiling, Mallory went back to driving, where, as far as she could see, all hell was breaking loose. Thank goodness he'd never asked her to deal with that stick shift again.

Putting one hand over her eyes, as if to shade them from sun, Amy turned to study Mallory's profile. At the beginning, she hadn't even *liked* him. He'd infuriated her. Now, she wanted to open him like a new book and read every line, cover to cover.

"You're staring. Please stop or or I'll run off the road."

With a little laugh, she turned back to the countryside. On either side, vineyards stretched as far as the eye could see. But most of the crops had been harvested and the trees bent over the braces, gnarled and spent.

"Sure would give a penny for your thoughts, Amy," Mallory drawled after a few moments. She'd been studying his hands.

Another perfect part.

Amy fingered the crinkled wrapper of the chocolate bar. "Just thinking we should be careful."

Mallory stiffened. "About what? I could have fixed us both a bourbon and peach tea in the time it took to get that condom on last night. The pharmacy in Venice better have the large pack. We destroyed more than one, as I recall. Is that a problem?"

"No, not at all. Besides, that's not the kind of safe I mean." No need to explain why birth control wasn't necessary. "In that department, yes, we're safe."

"Well, what then?" Mallory downshifted.

"Let's just take our time." What else could she say? "Don't hurt me like the last guy?" How pathetic. She was never doing pathetic again.

They were coming into the Piazza Roma, where they would drop off their rental car. Made her a little sad. The car held so many memories.

But Venice? Head swiveling, she drank in this outer edge of the city. The piazza hummed with activity—a jumble of cars, baggage, and travelers babbling in different languages. Sucking in a deep breath of the crisp morning air, she smiled.

Venice, city of romance. And she was here with a handsome man from Savannah. What could top this?

"I'll be right back." Pointing to the sign for the rental company, Amy was out of the car in a flash, eager to have something to do, something she could control. Because her feelings for Mallory?

Totally out of control.

After angling the car into a tight spot, Mallory watched Amy disappear into the car rental office. Struck him that it had been at least twenty-four hours since he'd thought of the custom BMW in Chad's showroom. He wasn't answering his cousin's calls. Finally he'd even turned his phone off except for the calls to Miriam.

What would Amy think if she ever knew about this crazy bet? Mallory's hands tightened on the ridges of the molded steering wheel. Hadn't she been lied to enough?

He liked her. *Really* liked her. And he liked her family.

The Shaw women felt so authentic. Mallory had exciting plans for them, well, after due diligence was done on both the jewelry enterprise and the niche T-shirt business. And at the end of the day, he didn't give two hoots and one holler what his board thought.

He drummed his fingers on the steering wheel. Last night had been incredible.

Business? The word felt hollow.

The week had become more than business, but for the life of him, Mallory couldn't put a name on everything he was feeling. He shifted in his seat to avoid the reflection of the sun on the hood. When Amy swirled from the door of the office, his heart felt too big for his chest. The sun caught her burnished curls as she jogged toward the car—so vital, so sexy in her mini skirt and white T-shirt. A warmth churned through his chest into his gut, as welcome as the frothy Italian coffee.

"Hey, handsome. Ready?" She knocked at the window.

"You bet." Jumping from the car, Mallory loped to the back and dragged the luggage out.

Within minutes, they were sprinting for the water taxi. The ride in the vaporetto would give him the time he needed to pull his thoughts into their usual logical order.

Stationed along the Riva del Vine, only steps from the Rialto Bridge, historic Hotel Marconi suggested a Venice of more prosperous times with its heavy-but-worn brocade drapes and intricately carved period furniture, marked by time and many visitors. From the nubile statuary in the lobby to the lush roses cascading from vases on the side tables, the hotel projected the opulence of an earlier era.

Upstairs, their room carried the Venetian theme even further with tinted mirrors and gilt sconces. Although Miriam had asked about changing this reservation when Mallory called her about Florence, he hesitated to meddle with too many of Amy's plans. This was, after all, her trip and she had put a great deal of thought into it.

How had that numbskull ever let her get away?

One man's folly can be another man's treasure.

Treasure. That suited Amy perfectly.

"Another great choice, Amy," Mallory marveled after the porter had left. He tried to forget that this room had been intended for a honeymoon with another man. Two twin beds were covered in gold brocade comforters. They should have called ahead. "One problem."

"At least they look a little wider than the ones in Florence." Surveying the beds, she nibbled on her lower lip.

"Not that wide." Mallory started shoving the beds together, while Amy pushed from the other side.

"What's on the agenda for today?" Skirting the beds, Mallory moved closer. Long afternoon ahead.

"Seeing the city?" Cute and coy, she tilted her head.

"Lots of history in Venice," he agreed.

Edging closer, Amy played with the buttons on his blue polo. Her eyelids flagged, tugging at his stomach and all points south when she fell against him like room temperature provolone. "You're so right. The palace, the campanile, who knows what else."

Her body started speaking to his. He liked the conversation.

"People would kill to be in our position. I mean, in Venice."

"Absolutely."

"They would be grabbing their maps and heading for the Piazza San Marco," he mumbled between kisses. Her neck was so soft. When he nibbled at her right ear, she shuddered. Lord, the woman was so responsive.

"So sexy when you say that." A delighted smile any man would cherish danced across her lips. "Piazza…whatever. We should go there."

"We most certainly should." Gently pushing her onto the bed, Mallory ran his hands up her legs and reached for the zipper on her skirt. "Any man in his right mind would be…"

"Stepping out?" she asked, lifting her hips.

"Exactly." Slowly, Mallory slid the skirt down to Amy's ankles, giving himself ample time to admire another delectable black thong. "We have other priorities."

Throwing her head back, Amy kicked her shorts to the floor. "Sure do."

Grabbing the collar of his polo, she pulled him to her. How he did enjoy her unexpected passion. Their kiss began slow and soft. But not for long. That ride from Florence had been so damn long.

"You taste like that chocolate you were munching." This must be what it was like to be plunged into a vat of melted chocolate.

"Um, so good," Amy murmured, hands tugging his shirt up and off. "Decadent." When she fanned her hands over his chest, her slender fingers sent fire blazing across his skin. Pulling back, he took in her flushed face, closed eyes, and parted lips.

"But you didn't share. The chocolate, that is," he reminded her, patting one finger against the nose that could look so pert and sassy.

Her green eyes blinked wide and then narrowed. "Was that naughty?"

He nodded. "Very. The time has come for sharing."

His hands slipped under her T-shirt, palming the pert tips of her breasts before he tugged the shirt off. He made short work of the lacy bra, wanting the full weight of her breasts in his hands.

"Ah, yes." Mallory noted the appreciative gleam in her eyes as he tugged and tightened his fingers. Her moans guided his exploration. Thongs were pretty but could get in the way. Slowly, he stripped the bit of lace from her legs. With a sigh, Amy settled against the pillows, an expectant smile tilting the corners of her lips.

By that time his briefs were long gone. When her hands reached for him, Mallory thought he would lose it right there. He stretched out beside her. "Do you like appetizers before dinner?"

"Of course. Why?"

"Well, Miss Amy, consider this a first course."

Three hours later, they sat at Harry's Bar down on the Grand Canal, sipping bellinis, the Italian specialty concocted with peach nectar and champagne. The chill of the crushed ice made her teeth ache. They had to wait thirty minutes to get a seat and filled the time with blatant PDA. Amy didn't care who saw or noticed. None of the parents from school would be here.

Easier to be a babe in another country with no students or parents.

"Thank you for the flowers." When Amy awakened from a needed nap, a gorgeous bouquet of pink gerbera daisies sat in the ice bucket on the side table. Apparently Mallory had slipped out to one of the flower stalls while she slept. Where he got the energy after their torrid early afternoon session was beyond her. Amy still felt limp, with a few mild aches in all the right places. As long as she could walk, she was fine.

This must be how a wanton woman would feel—satisfied and a little sore.

"What's that Cheshire cat grin about?" Mallory's blue eyes warmed above the rim of the glass.

"Nothing. Everything."

After the much needed nap—being a babe could be exhausting—they got dressed and headed for the Piazza San Marco. They even tagged along behind a group touring the Doges Palace with a guide. Wasn't this why she'd included Venice—the history? The ceilings of the palace soared above them, walls and arches adorned with intricate carvings and ancient tapestries. But overall, the palace was dark, as were the stories of the stern rule of the doges. What a relief it had been to escape back into the sunlight.

"So what did you think of the palace?" Amy asked as they sipped their bellinis. "You were pretty quiet."

Taking one of her hands, Mallory began to play with her fingers. "I have a low tolerance for large musty museums, palaces, forts. Not my thing. But since I'm with you...well, I'm willing to tag along."

That darn red flag went up. "So you didn't come on this trip necessarily to see Italy?"

When Mallory looked away, her heart contracted. "I would imagine that no one can ever get enough of Italy."

One week with no complications was beginning to feel hollow.

"The palace wasn't as interesting as the paintings in the Uffizi," Mallory said.

"Any paintings in particular?" Back to their teasing banter.

"Have to admit, I *am* partial to nudes."

She swallowed. "Figured that."

Mallory nodded knowingly, eyes flashing into blue heat. Her throat and lips felt parched, as if seared by a brush fire, and she tossed back what was left of her bellini.

Hands linked, they wandered out, stopping in various shops and kiosks that sold jewelry, blown glass pens with delicate writing paper, or first editions along with the latest best sellers. One kiosk on the walkway fronting the bay featured a wall of masks in bright blue, yellow or green—a dazzling display of color, adorned by feathers and ribbons that danced in the breeze sweeping off the canal.

"Mardi Gras! Aren't these wonderful?" The masks glittered in the sunlight, mysterious and playful.

"Look. Just matches your new dress." Mallory unhooked a gorgeous green mask with yellow sequins edging the openings for the eyes. Plumes of lime and aqua feathers along with long silk streamers of green and blue cascaded from one side.

Carefully, Amy slipped it over her hair.

"Very nice. Adds a bit of mystery." Mallory stepped back in appreciation.

"It doesn't feel like me." Staring at herself in the mirror, she felt dazed. Amy wanted to be this woman always.

And that scared the heck out of her.

On impulse, she grabbed a blue mask with a bright yellow and blue harlequin design and held it up to Mallory's face. But seeing his eyes peeking out from the mask chilled her. Quickly, she returned both masks to the display.

"Not a good color on me?"

"Didn't do you justice." Breaking away, she strolled toward the next booth. When Mallory caught up with her, he had bought the green mask. Oh, this wouldn't do. Mallory made decisions so quickly, while she agonized, weighing each option.

Then she stopped. Did she want to be a list maker? Did she want to be the woman who didn't go out for a beer with the other teachers because she had papers to grade?

"Thank you." Clutching the bag to her chest, she knew she'd keep this mask forever.

After wandering around aimlessly and watching a mime dressed all in white perform at one of the interior squares, they went back to freshen up for dinner. The concierge had suggested a casual restaurant that sat on the canal in front of the Hotel Marconi. Mallory didn't see any point in consulting a guidebook to find something more exotic.

If the phone rang, he checked to make sure it wasn't Amy's mother or aunt but he was not answering Chad's calls. His head just couldn't go there.

A good choice, the restaurant was intimate, but he hardly knew what he was eating. His mind spun, filled with questions.

One thing had become clear. He wanted more than one week with Amy. And his need had nothing to do with the terms of a wager.

As dusk settled over the darkening waters of the canals after dinner, Mallory and Amy strolled hand in hand toward the Piazza San Marco, where the music of a stringed quartet floated over the square. They settled at a table at one of the cafes clustered at the edges of the piazza. Fat pigeons toddled about the square, pecking for crumbs.

"Haven't heard a thing from Caitlin." Thin lines of worry creased Amy's brow.

Mallory chucked her gently under the chin. "Maybe they're otherwise engaged. Like us."

"Could be. She's not like me…"

He caught her hand. "You're very different but both special. And she is devoted to you." In some ways, he felt Caitlin had helped his cause.

"Really?" Settling back in her chair, she laughed softly. Her contentment pleased him.

The waiter brought the wine. Mallory could not remember when he'd felt this satisfied and it had nothing to do with the food.

Dark clouds scudded across a night sky. The end of the trip loomed.

"Doesn't everything feel special here?" Amy's glance swept the darkening piazza.

When he expanded his chest with a sigh that came from his toes, Thornton Enterprises seemed distant and unimportant. With a instrumental flourish, the quartet launched into a spirited tango.

"Dance?" Eager to have her in his arms, Mallory sprang to his feet.

Amy gripped the arms of her chair. "Oh, Mallory. I can't tango!"

Four couples had moved onto the piazza, away from the tables. One duo began to tango, their liquid movements defying their heavy leather sandals. An older couple initiated a slower, more sedate tango, backs rigid and arms in position. The others merely swayed to the music.

He'd be damned if he was going to miss this dance, even though he hadn't a clue where to put his feet. He smiled down at Amy. "Can you lean? I can't tango either, but I lean well. Sometimes even in time to the music."

Amy's wistful eyes followed the dancers.

Prying one hand from the chair, Mallory gently tugged her to her feet. With a timid smile, she folded nicely into his body.

Just as she would in his life.

A plan had begun to formulate in his mind. Amy's head rested soft on his shoulder as they swayed across the uneven stones. Others soon joined them, but for that moment, they were the only two people on the piazza and they belonged together.

"Isn't this the best, Mallory?"

He cupped his hand over hers, the one flat against his heart. "The very best."

"Could we leave?"

"My thought exactly."

Chapter 20

"We really need to go to Murano today?" Mallory asked. Staying in bed seemed so right. Amy's skin felt soft and the bed warm. Room service made perfect sense.

Hair deliciously mussed, she gave him a stern glance. "The glass blowers are known worldwide."

"Love it when you talk teacher to me."

Murano. In the foyer of his Savannah mansion sat an enormous piece of green Murano glass atop an ebony pedestal. Overhead hung a stunning blue and green Chihuly chandelier, his mother's favorite.

Amy had not shown any curiosity about his family or his home. Sympathetic? Yes. Curious? Not really. Rhonda has just about demanded an inventory of the Savannah mansion after the first time they'd slept together.

Spooning deeper into the arch of Mallory's body, she sighed. Then she grabbed one of her infernal travel guides from the nightstand and began to fumble through the pages. "That is why we came, right?"

Mallory's veins turned to ice. He could never tell Amy why he'd come on this junket to Italy. The corporation? The luxury car?

Looking back, he felt like a damn fool. That night in the

Oglethorpe Club was an eternity ago.

"Murano it is." Throwing back the covers, he headed for the shower. He needed time to clear his head. Time to strategize.

When Mallory and Amy reached the bay in front of the Doges Palace, they hopped aboard a tour boat headed for Murano. The farther out they got, the better the view. Mallory pointed to a large cruise ship that sat at anchor. "Ever taken a cruise?"

"No." Amy squinted at the huge liner.

"We'll have to do that some day."

"Happy talk." Pulling away, she frowned.

"What was that?"

"Nothing."

"No really, Amy. I'd like to know."

Just then, the excursion boat pulled along the weathered pier of Murano, and they all filed off. Shuffling onto the dock in back of an older couple, Mallory sank into troubled thoughts. Was Amy keeping secrets from him?

Guilt squelched that suspicion. Wasn't he harboring secrets of his own? Another glance toward the cruise ship pushed everything else from his mind.

Perfect. Crazy, but perfect.

Taking Amy's hand, he led her into the colorful town, where pink, blue and yellow storefronts offered a firsthand glimpse of artists at work. Her breezy aqua top and mini skirt were so girly, so her, as were those cute blue sandals.

If he did meet his goal—and he was becoming more determined by the hour—he wondered what stone to give her for a wedding gift. Would it be jade, the color of her eyes when she became so serious…or aquamarine to remind them of the day she leapt into the bay at Monterosso? His showrooms carried only the highest quality stones. Nothing else would do for Amy.

Morning sun bounced off the colorful stucco facades of buildings, cooled by a refreshing breeze from the bay. Stores closest to the dock quickly filled with tourists. They moved past, finally entering an empty shop. At the back stood a middle-aged guy with a ponytail. A sturdy chap, the artist braced his feet wide while he worked. Mouth set and eyes protected by goggles, he twirled a long metal pole in an open furnace glowing with white heat. Although the artist wore thick gloves, the scars on his arms weren't recent. This guy had probably spent years perfecting his art.

"There are times when I'm in awe of the artist in the front lines," Mallory said as the man put his mouth to the end of the blowpipe, cheeks rounding with the effort.

Amy wheeled around, eyes suddenly cool and guarded. "Are you talking about the artists you meet in your own work?"

So it had come to that. All week he'd been dancing around what he did for a living. Mallory certainly didn't want to be cast in the same light as her idiot fiancé, but this wasn't the time to explain. When was the right time to tell a woman you're worth millions?

"Right, with my jewelry store." He let it go at that.

Amy picked up a vase shaped like a pear. "Will you look at this? So beautiful."

Slowly, she ran one finger along the lips that tucked into a v in both front and back. The glass was a delicate pale pink that deepened in the folds as the design tightened. An arrow of need lanced through Mallory's body.

Everything about Amy was so damn sexy.

"I'll take it." Then, at her startled look, he added, "Good for Christmas. Don't you agree?"

"Christmas." Her smile faded.

"Lordy, I never know what to give my staff." Although she joined him as they chose colors, something was off. What had changed her mood?

By that time, the glass blower's wife had joined them. Mallory gave her shipping instructions for his lot.

"Oh, you can just put mine in a bag," Amy said quickly. "I want to look at them."

"Sure? They'll be heavy."

"When we get back home, I'm going to line them up on the bureau and just remember…how beautiful they are." A muscle moved in her throat.

Her enthusiasm touched him. The morning felt so damned domestic, like they were a couple. He almost felt drugged by complacency as they drifted back to the boat.

When they reached the Piazza San Marco, Amy made a quick call to Caitlin and they set up plans to meet for lunch.

"Don't mean to be avoiding you," she told her sister.

"Don't worry about it. Why don't I give you a call when we find a restaurant?"

"Sounds like a plan." Her sister's voice sounded sleepy, even though it was almost noon. Probably still in bed. Amy's bag weighed heavy on her arm.

Hadn't they spent the morning wisely? But another part of her wished they'd lounged in the room. Time was short. When he mentioned Christmas, a hole had opened up inside her.

Over the past few days, Amy's life had gone haywire. Her travel chum had become more important than the trip. As they strolled the cobblestones of Venice, a sadness fell over her.

The end was in sight.

The end of her trip and the end of her travel chum.

After leaving the boat, they'd wandered down one of the narrow streets that led off the piazza. Mallory's arm kept her close, and she let her head fall onto his shoulder. Shadows became narrow as the sun climbed overhead.

How she wished he'd say something, but none of the happy talk, please. Men did it all the time—another topic for McKenna and Vanessa as they sat in Petersen's Ice Cream Parlor. Men would paint a picture of the future, like an insurance policy they never intended to cash. Mallory hadn't shared any details about his work and his life. Surely that indicated that he saw no future for them. Whatever they had was just for this week.

A babe wouldn't care.

Her steps faltered.

But she did.

A capricious wind tunneled through the tight buildings, playing havoc with Mallory's hair. The boys she taught would finger it into stiff spikes with goo or round it into a smooth cap. Not Mallory.

The man lived in comfortable certainty about himself.

So why did she feel so uncertain?

Who was Mallory Schuster? She wished she had a computer handy so she could Google him. But what did it matter? Just one more day.

The street had taken them into another smaller piazza with an outdoor cafe. Cozy tables were arranged under a green awning.

"Good?" Mallory turned to her.

"Perfect." Checking the street name on the worn stones of the corner building, she called Caitlin.

"Amy, would you be furious if we copped out on lunch?"

A waitress arrived and handed Amy a menu. "Of course not. After all, we see each other all the time."

"Kurt and I don't want to mess up your time with Mallory."

"It's not like that." Amy glanced across the table. Lips pursed, Mallory was studying the menu.

"It *could* be like that, Amy."

"Maybe."

"Do something wild and crazy, okay?" Her sister sounded so darn frustrated.

"I will. I am," she insisted, plucking at the edge of the menu. "See you at home, Caitlin, or maybe we'll end up on the same flight back."

"Yeah, well, we're taking a later flight out. Kurt changed the plans. Wanted to spend more time here." Amy could hear the smile in Caitlin's voice and knew Kurt was right there.

Her heart hammered just thinking about returning to the states.

"Mallory is a great guy. Do *not* let that man get away."

What her sister really meant was *do not screw this up, Amy*.

But there was nothing to screw up. Was there?

"Have a good flight back, Cait. Talk to you later."

Mallory's brows lifted as Amy tucked her phone away. "Change of plans?"

"Caitlin's not coming."

Mallory's eyelids drooped with sly understanding. "I understand."

The waiter came, and they ordered.

"So, what should we do this afternoon?" Amy asked as they waited for their salads. "See the sites?"

"Maybe we should rest up a bit?" When Mallory pursed his lips, memories coursed through her.

She knew the power of those lips, and her skin prickled. "Thought we might take in La Fenice. You know, the oldest opera house. Burned down in the 1800s. Of course, they eventually rebuilt it. Very well known."

The waiter arrived with their order. Bits of the historical facts she'd studied for months came back, and she tossed them out like seasonings.

"Or we could go back to the hotel for a bit," he suggested once the waiter retreated. Mallory's tone suggested they might go back to tidy up a bit. His smile held devious intent as he cut into the chicken strips on his salad.

"Really?" She dashed more olive oil on her lettuce.

"You know, check on the room."

"Make sure it's still there." Amy played with her fork, suddenly not hungry. At least, not for chicken salad. "Or we could visit the church of San Polo that houses the painting of the Last Supper. We shouldn't leave without seeing that."

"Mold," Mallory offered with an exaggerated sniff. "Those old churches. Maybe what we need is a little rest."

"Or the Bridge of Sighs. We can't go back without seeing this bridge. All the prisoners, poor things, would cross this bridge on their way to prison.

"Why would anyone bury themselves in a dark dingy covered bridge on a day like today? I have a much better idea."

"What would that be?" Her imagination brought a damp rush.

Leaning so close that she could see a trace of vinaigrette on his lips, Mallory chucked her gently under the chin. "I have a surprise for you. Eat quickly, *cara*."

With a shiver, she picked up her fork.

Cara. Tossed about in markets and restaurants with seductive abandon, the word now magically applied to her.

After he'd settled the bill, Mallory hustled her back to the Piazza San Marco. "This surprise will be quintessentially Venice. Trust me."

"Are we going back to the islands?" Funny how she enjoyed his spontaneous moments. For years her schedule had ensured success. Now? Not so sure.

"No more islands today." The mystery deepened, along with something else kept deep in her heart.

Chapter 21

Gondolas sat moored along the piers, manned by young men in striped T-shirts and flat-brimmed straw hats. The boats rocked gently on the water. Amy's delight warmed his heart. After a quick conversation with a gondolier, Mallory ushered her into a bright red boat.

"Just like the movies!" Amy cried, reclining on a gently worn cushion. "I feel like Katherine Hepburn!"

"The Rialto Bridge," Mallory told the gondolier. One push and they were off. "Seeing Venice from a gondola is a must."

"So you've done this before?" Her smile faltered.

Damn. "No, ma'am, as I live and breathe, this is my first gondola ride." Mallory expelled a tight breath.

The young man maneuvered the prow of the long craft into one of the shaded waterways that threaded through Venice. With slow grace, they glided past aging mansions and under arched walkways.

With Amy nestled next to him, Mallory struggled to concentrate on the scenery, but his mind chattered. How he wanted to drop this ridiculous pretense of being Mallory Schuster. Timing was everything. First, he wanted to be more sure he wasn't in this alone. Amy seemed to have feelings for him. The tightness in his chest felt familiar and usually accompanied any new acquisition.

A few days ago, he would not have believed he was considering this next step. Like a little boy, he wanted more. More time, more everything…with Amy. Downright amazing how the reservations following his divorce had been wiped out by the delightful time he'd had with her family.

The prospect of losing control of Thornton Enterprises would be enough to put fire to any man's heels. But that wasn't it. He didn't want to go home to the empty mansion. Didn't want one more Christmas of booking a room in some luxury hotel in the Caribbean. Not after Amy.

As they continued deeper into the waterways, the young gondolier extolled the wonders of various historical points of interest. Amy didn't seem to be listening. Instead, she lazed in Mallory's arms like a magnolia blossom, beautiful in her simplicity. He nuzzled a favorite warm spot, just below her right ear. "You are so delicious."

"Mmm. You too." She cupped his chin in her soft hand.

He wanted to be held like this forever.

The boat nosed into the Grand Canal.

"Almost home," he whispered.

"Finally," she murmured, soft as the cooing of doves tucked up in the crumbling eaves of the Venetian mansions. She shuddered when his tongue flicked her ear lobe.

The Rialto Bridge loomed above, and they glided to a halt under its shadow. When the boat nudged the aged bricks, the gondolier jumped onto the landing. After helping Amy up, Mallory pushed some bills into the young man's hand and waved good-bye.

They strolled over the bridge, hand in hand. A sense of peace fell over him, such a contrast to the funk he'd been in lately.

Funk. A Chad word. His cousin was probably royally pissed off because Mallory hadn't been taking his calls.

He should be grateful to Chad. The vacation has been his idea. Chad's casual comment that he might marry his travel chum and meet the board's demands had been tossed out as a joke.

Now? He'd never felt like this with Rhonda. Never.

The lobby of Hotel Marconi was empty, with only the concierge busy at the desk. Since the elevator was parked on an upper floor, they headed for the stairs. "Have you thought about dinner?" she asked as she took the lead.

"Not really." He rested one hand on her wonderfully rounded backside as they climbed the stairs.

Amy's surprised chortle reached right into his manhood and squeezed. Was this the same shy woman he'd startled on the plane at JFK? Her laugh cinched tight when his hand trailed up her inner thigh, enjoying what he found there.

"They might have cameras on these stairs." She swatted at his hand playfully.

"Teacher talk again?" Finally reaching their floor, he chased her down the hall and jammed their keycard in the lock. "You know the consequences."

"Private detention after school?" She threw him a sultry look.

He chuckled. "Right. Studying *my* favorite subject."

With a giggle, she twined her arms around his neck and they stumbled through the open door. He slammed it behind them, tossed the keycard on the desk and twisted out of his jacket. Amy's hands fumbled with his belt buckle and he tried to tug her gauzy top over her head without ripping it. Clothes landed in a pile on the floor, and Amy fell back against the pillow. Her hair formed a radiant halo around her head.

"Definitely Rossetti. You'd put any of his paintings to shame." Mallory paused to appreciate the vision. Fanned on the pillow case, Amy's blonde hair shimmered against her porcelain skin. The room lay suffused in the golden glow of late afternoon, but she provided her own radiance. After stepping out of his briefs, he kicked them to the side and dove onto the bed.

When he leveraged himself halfway over her body, every curve of her body came alive. Amy had this way of moving her hips in rhythm even before rhythm was definitely called for. "Are you teasing me?"

She lifted one brow. "Do I have to?"

"Are you kidding?"

Her hands pleased his body with gentle but certain strokes. When Amy made love, there was nothing tentative about it.

"Am I hurting you?" she asked suddenly, her hands stopping.

"Not at all, *cara*," Mallory whispered against her lips.

Amy helped him unroll the condom. Somewhere, a cell phone rang. Mallory thought he'd turned the damn thing off. He was definitely technologically challenged.

Amy's body grew stilled. "Who the heck calls you all the time?"

"No one. Do. Not. Stop," Mallory ground out the words, accompanied by some serious thrusting. Why wasn't Chad checking on his showrooms or taking Mirandah shopping?

When Amy woke up, they were tangled in the sheets, legs overlapping and arms entwined. Snug upon his shoulder, Amy had one hand flat on his chest. Mallory's eyes were half open. Anyone who thought blue was a cool color should see his eyes after making love.

Falling back, she took in the Venetian touches in their room. Lordy, was this what the beautiful people did all the time when they traveled?

Beautiful people. Mallory fell into that category. Somehow, she just knew. His picture probably appeared in society magazines she'd never seen.

She didn't want to know. Not really.

For one week, he'd been perfect.

Was that enough? It had to be.

Her heart pinched.

Mallory curled a length of her hair around his finger. "You're...fun, Amy."

Fun? Was the bitter taste in her mouth disappointment?

Mallory pulled her tighter, and her arm reached across the amazing breadth of his chest, as if that could hold him. But she couldn't. He wasn't a student at her command.

"That was truly amazing."

She dragged her mind from the edge of the dreadful abyss. "Who knew that marble sink would hold my weight?"

"*Cara.*" She melted into that word while he chuckled. "*I* can hold your weight."

A while later, they made it to the shower. Her laughter turned to moans while he lathered her with rich, almond scented soap. Mallory would get an A for thoroughness. Later, while he shaved again, she called McKenna.

"I need help," she sputtered when her friend picked up. "Are you seeing patients?"

"In between. You sound terrible. What's going on?"

"I don't know. I think I'm in love."

"That's terrific." Delight and surprise lifted McKenna's voice.

"But he hasn't said anything, McKenna. That's my problem."

"Do *not* make this a problem." Now McKenna sounded like the teacher. "Give him time. Enjoy…be a babe."

She gulped. The water had shut off in the bathroom. Mallory was trying to sing "Volare," and she smiled as she said good-bye. Tucking her phone away, she heard his mobile phone go off and was tempted to answer. But that just felt so wrong. Besides, she had to get dressed.

One hour later, they were strolling toward the piazza.

Certain parts of her body ached. When she was back in the classroom, she would long for this welcome discomfort. All she would have on those cold Chicago days were her usual monthly pains and problems. A stern reminder that no man could give her what she really wanted. How could there be another man after Mallory?

Shivering, she tugged her purple woven shawl tighter around her black sweater. Dry leaves chased down the street in front of them. Fall was coming.

They found a restaurant next to one of the canals down near the Doges Palace. Wide windows afforded a great view. The fish was tender, the salad crisp. She tasted textures but not flavors as they ate in silence. Their last night. The words echoed in her head like the bells from the campanile in the piazza.

"You're so quiet." Mallory leaned toward her. The waiter had cleared the table, and they were lingering over coffee. "Have I exhausted you?"

Her glance fell on the dark bay, the lights of Murano winking in the distance. Had that just been today?

"There's so much we don't know about each other, Mallory." Amy regretted her words the moment she'd said them.

Mallory's shoulders tensed, and then he exhaled with a shake of his head. "You're right. I learned a lot about you and your family over the past week."

"You were a good sport about it." What other man would want to share a week with a woman's relatives?

"You probably don't know this because, well, you've had them all your life. Your family is real," Mallory said with a puzzling earnestness.

Amy ran one finger around the rim of her coffee cup. She hadn't touched a drop. "This week—it's been great. I'd recommend Travel Chums to anyone looking for a good man to share a trip." There. Didn't she sound worldly and sophisticated?

Mallory's face drained. "Time to come clean, Amy…"

Oh. My. God. She held up both hands. "No need, Mallory.

Really."

Was he married? Engaged? She didn't want to know. Her heart squeezed.

"Please, Amy." He caught her fingers with one hand. "I'm not a poor traveler who had to troll Travel Chums for a partner to share travel expenses."

"I suspected as much." She tried to tug her hand free. "That doesn't matter. You don't have to tell me any more."

Mallory's grip tightened. "It matters to me. For heaven's sake, will you listen? I own, well, quite a large business. Not just one jewelry store, Amy."

"Fine. Good...I guess."

"Whole string of them, actually." Briefly he filled her in, and the words crumbled over her like the stonework in Vernazza. When he got to the part about Miriam Schuster being his assistant, the pebbles shifted from her feet to her stomach. She was right back in that locker room, deception thick in the air instead of steam.

"Amy?" Frowning, Mallory signed the check. "Are you all right?"

She fought to push through a wall of disappointment. "It's just a lot to take in, Mallory. I have this thing about truth."

Like the truth she hadn't shared with Jason until it was almost too late? Was she being a hypocrite? She sprang to her feet, the chair scraping the floor in loud protest.

"I do too, or I wouldn't be telling you this." Taking her elbow, Mallory steered her toward the door.

"It really doesn't matter now, does it?" Their final evening together. Amy wrapped her arms around her waist as they pushed outside. *If I can just hold it together for one more night.* The night air held the foreboding of autumn, and mist coated her cheeks. Or was she crying?

She'd never heard of Thornton Enterprises. What did it matter? She cared about the man, not the company. When Mallory tried to put his arm around her, she twisted away. Finally he stuck his hands into the pockets of his khaki chinos.

Compared to this week, her life had played out in black and white. This past week, she'd lived in vibrant color. All because of Mallory.

She loved him. Funny, considerate, charming.

She loved all of him, no matter who he was.

The lights from the cruise ship blinked across the dark bay. They walked until the Piazza San Marco lay before them, musicians setting up to play. Mallory and Amy took a table and eventually danced in the moonlight. The song was "Strangers in the Night," and it had never sounded so sad, the kind of sad that could haunt you forever. Tightening her arms around his neck, she laid her head on his shoulder.

Just had to hold him one last time.

"Amy, please don't be angry. I never meant to hurt you," he whispered.

Anger jerked her back. "Mallory, it's different for me, okay? I'll always remember this...trip. For me, there isn't a string of trips. Probably not a chance to come back. Just *this.*"

Her favorite honeymoon. So different from what she planned.

No one could plan anything this perfect.

But of course she couldn't say *that*. The words lodged in her throat with the certainty of regret.

"My God. Do you think I won't remember?" Eyes earnest, almost pleading, he unleashed a wobbly smile. "Lordy, hasn't it been crazy, Amy? Crazy and wonderful."

"Yep. Right." Clutching his arms, she didn't want to ever let him go.

"Let's get married tonight." His arms tightened.

"What…what did you say?"

"Let's get married. We should, Amy."

"Oh, Mallory." What was he saying?

He gave her a little shake. "Is that a yes or a no?"

And he kissed her. Kissed her into yes.

What was she waiting for?

Amy threw herself over the ledge of her caution…and it felt glorious.

"Yes. Let's," she gasped, coming up for air. "But, Mallory, there's just one thing."

Her words trailed after him as he broke and took off across the piazza, pulling her behind him. She had to tell him, didn't she? But he would not slow down.

Caitlin's words rang in her ears. She would tell her to "let loose." McKenna and Vanessa might be thrilled beyond belief that Amy was, after all, a babe.

Heart beating in her throat, she started to run. Mallory headed toward the water taxis.

"I have to call Caitlin."

"Good thinking. They can be our witnesses." He glanced out at the lights sparkling on the cruise ship.

One call to Caitlin and Kurt and her sister's loud shrieks made this craziness even more real. While they waited near the water taxis for her sister to arrive, Amy and Mallory cuddled and did things that other lovers do in Venice. They just don't do them in public.

Finally, her sister and her boyfriend arrived, breathless and eyes bright with excitement. The four of them jumped aboard a water taxi.

"You sure about this?" Caitlin whispered as the boat cut a straight path through water.

"Positive."

"Good." Caitlin squeezed her elbow. "Wait 'til Mom hears."

Apparently Mallory had made some calls. When they arrived, the captain was waiting in his state room. Low lighting caught the glint of the gold trim on his black uniform. A female officer pushed a bouquet of white calla lilies into Amy's hands. The ceremony was short but quite conclusive.

This had to be a movie of another woman's life.

Amy was married...on the trip that was to have been her honeymoon, and she was married to a man she loved dearly.

The fact that he might not feel the same? She would deal with it later. He must have some feelings for her, especially after the hurtful stories about Rhonda. Why else would he have done this?

"Happy?" Mallory asked as they returned to shore.

"Very." She closed her mind and listened to her heart.

Chapter 22

As the water taxi headed toward Marco Polo Airport, Mallory should have felt damn near ecstatic, but he had some loose ends to tie up. And he hated loose ends.

The night before had gone well. Of course Amy would be moving to Savannah, and her family could visit anytime, especially since Thornton Enterprises would be doing business with them. How fortunate that Louise and Caitlin both had cottage industries. The mentoring aspect should appeal to his board. And if not? He really didn't give a damn.

Still, had he overlooked something? He pressed his fingertips into closed eyelids, but when he opened them again, the fog hadn't cleared.

"Sleepy?" Amy peered up at him.

"A little." Mallory massaged his new wife's neck. The knots in her shoulders resisted. When the taxi hit a wave, icy spray splashed them. Amy gasped. He'd be glad to get back on dry land.

Out of touch for a week, he craved action. Decision-making.

"We should talk, Mallory."

His stomach plummeted. The boat slapped another oncoming wave.

"Can it wait? We're almost at the airport." Up ahead, the lights blasted the darkness. He was too brain dead for a discussion. He'd already put two calls in to Chad, but his cousin wasn't picking up. Straining through the darkness, he kept his eyes on the lights.

After returning from the cruise ship, Caitlin and Kurt had gone their own way. Amy had called Louise and Aunt Em. Mallory could hear them squealing from the other side of the room. Sharing the news was fun. How he did love Amy's glow, and he looked forward to seeing Louise and Aunt Em again. But he needed to get in touch with Chad, and that had to be a private conversation.

When they finally fell asleep, they'd slept so soundly they'd nearly missed the water taxi. Amy had been quiet as they rushed to leave the hotel. Now she wanted to talk? First, he had some things to straighten out on his end.

Chad could never mention the bet to Amy. What would her reaction be if she thought their marriage was the result of a wager with his cousin? Although his new bride seemed sensible, women had their limits.

And that wasn't the situation. Far from it. He was crazy about her. The fact that Mallory was almost knocked speechless by a woman at this stage of the game? Land sakes, that was downright amazing.

He was obsessed with Amy. Even when he was with her, he thought about her. The way the sun made her hair glisten. How her hip curved like a gently sloping sand dune at Hilton Head. And that laugh…

She was smart, charming, and fun.

And now she was his wife.

So much lay ahead. Of course, she had to return to Chicago for a while. She'd explained that she was under contract and planned on sitting down with her principal about what could be done. Given a little time, everything would fall into place.

The water taxi deposited them at the dock of the airport. Mallory quickly engaged porters. Amy continued to look pinched and dazed. Poor thing.

As they settled into their seats thirty minutes later, the mood on the plane was subdued. Tempers short, travelers grumpy. Full flight. How he wished he'd had Miriam change their tickets to first class. Amy insisted that Mallory take the aisle seat in their center row of five. On her other side a young man wore headphones. No cheerful Ethel this time to lighten the mood.

Mallory flipped up the armrest the moment they got settled. Stretching his legs into the aisle, he still felt cramped. Amy looked uncomfortable. Then she sighed and offered him a crooked smile. His spirits lifted.

Everything would be fine.

This felt so right.

This was all wrong. Amy fussed with her seatbelt and adjusted the air nozzles overhead. What had she been thinking? The certificate in her luggage said she was married. If only it really meant something. There was just so much unfinished business, including one very important detail. After hearing Mallory's sad tales of life as an only child, Amy imagined having his own family was very important. What would he think when she told him? A heavy weight pressed into her chest until she wondered if she'd ever breathe freely again.

There had been no talk of love from Mallory. Of course, Jason had never been upfront about his feelings either. Still, she wasn't going to be the first one to bring it up.

"Penny for your thoughts?" Mallory fixed her with those blue eyes that could narrow into laser beams. He'd gone into his CEO mode on the way to the airport. All authority and organization, he snapped orders right and left when they got to the dock. Did she even know this man? Now he squeezed her hand. "What are you frowning about?"

"Just thinking about…what a great trip we had." Her eyes fell on her bare ring finger.

"We'll take care of a ring when we get home."

"No need." Embarrassed, Amy curled her left hand into a ball.

"Don't be silly. You're my wife."

This wasn't about a diamond. She'd made a commitment to a stranger who'd answered her ad for a travel chum. But she hadn't been totally honest with him. Maybe she needed a lesson plan, like the ones used in the classroom, to straighten all this out. Exhausted by the committee in her head, she couldn't get comfortable in this seat.

"No room at all." Mallory fumed and fidgeted. Angling his body, he was like a senior trying to cram himself into the lab chairs in freshman study hall.

"Let's fix that." Pushing herself up, Amy studied the seating.

"I'll be fine," he insisted between gritted teeth.

"There are some free seats in the back if you want to stretch out."

"Really?" Crouching, he half stood.

"It might be the best for your back, you know." Amy ducked her head so he wouldn't see she was about to burst into tears.

For a minute, her new husband was perfectly still. Then he gathered his eyeshade and his blanket. "If you don't mind."

"Of course not." Plunking back into her seat, Amy yanked a magazine out of the seat pocket in front of her.

"Let me know if you need anything."

"Sure." The vacancy next to Amy felt wide as the ocean when Mallory walked away. At least now she had time to think.

Since her connecting flight left before his, Mallory planned to sit with her for a while. Maybe that would be a good time to talk things through. Head settled, Amy napped fitfully. The meal tasted like cardboard. Chicken, was it? Even the air felt dry and stale. The guy next to her kept bobbing his knees to his music. She fought the urge to still that knee with a firm hand.

Seemed like forever before the plane landed at JFK. When Mallory made his way back to Amy, he looked rested.

"All set?" Dropping into the seat, he took her hand.

"You bet." As ready as she'd ever be.

"Trust me?"

What did that mean? Amy managed a quick nod. "Yep. Sure."

Hadn't he saved her life…in more ways than one? Certainly they could work this out. Even if he didn't love her, he seemed to care for her. Instead of a fiancée who'd been kicked to the curb, she was an adventurous woman who'd traveled with a stranger. She'd fallen in love and gotten married. The wonder of it bloomed in her chest, warm and promising. For the past week she'd trusted this man with more than her heart. But she had to be honest about her situation. Any good marriage was founded on trust.

The landing felt bumpy, rattling luggage in the bins overhead. Everyone released a sigh of relief when the plane came to a stop. Exiting down the side aisle, Amy felt Mallory behind her. Steady. Strong. They would have time to talk. Somehow she would tell him that the sad facts. If he objected, well, their marriage could be quietly annulled.

Shameless as she was, she clung to a tiny thread of hope. Maybe he'd agree to adoption.

Mallory leaned closer. "I'll stay with you as long as I can before I head to my gate. Plenty of time to talk."

She released a pent up breath. "Good. I'd like that."

At the end of the ramp, a cluster of people craned their necks, searching for loved ones.

Amy filled with gratitude. After all, he'd given her so much during this past week. Wasn't this the man who had listened to her sad tale in Monterosso and comforted her? She smiled, remembering his threat to thrash Jason. How cute was that?

And now he was her husband.

"Oh, Mallory…" Heart overflowing, Amy half turned, one hand against his chest.

"Mallory!" The voice cut the air. "Buddy!"

Mallory's hands tightened on her shoulders as she twisted to stare at the man waving to her husband. With a pretty woman next to him, Mallory's friend had a distinguished air about him. Something metallic dangled from his hand.

"Who is that, Mallory?"

"Chad, my cousin." He began to push past her. Although he'd mentioned Chad, she didn't recall hearing he was meeting Mallory in New York. "Amy, no matter what, we'll work it out."

Amy's steps lagged. Other travelers edged around her while her heart went into free fall.

Whatever this was, it wasn't good. Chad's smile froze as Mallory approached. His hand closed over what looked like a key. The other woman glanced at Chad and then at Amy, her smile dissolving.

Above the commotion of arrival on a busy concourse, she heard Mallory say, "Deal's off, buddy. Deal is off."

Deal?

Chad's face paled. "You mean you don't want the car?"

Mallory edged her out of the main line of traffic. Perspiration had broken out on his forehead. One of his eyes twitched. "Chad, I'd like you to meet Amy, my wife. Amy, this is Chad, my best friend and cousin, who is sorely mistaken, although he doesn't know it yet. And this is Mirandah Fairchild."

"Glad to meet you, Amy."

Mirandah stepped forward, but Amy barely saw her extended hand. Her eyes were on Chad and the key fob.

"Mallory, you've been MIA, buddy." Chad's eyes got wider with each word. "Did you say married?"

"What's this about a car?" Amy's gaze remained glued to that key.

"Nothing." Mallory's lips barely moved.

Chad whisked both hands behind his back. "Just thought I'd come and meet you. Bad idea?"

Amy shook her head to clear it. "Could someone explain this to me, please?"

Mirandah's lips clamped firmly shut.

Mallory dipped his head, as if he were scooping up his courage. The tight smile made him look like a stranger. Other travelers streamed past them. Mirandah dragged Chad several feet away and began talking quietly to him, her head bobbing.

"Amy, I made a ridiculous bet with Chad. We're cousins and old friends. And we're guys. The wager was stupid." His eyes pleaded with her.

"How stupid?" Amy could hardly get the words out.

"Very stupid." The muscles worked in Mallory's throat, the strong column she had loved to kiss. Good grief, that seemed so long ago.

"Please explain."

His face fell. Disoriented, Amy felt abandoned, stranded in the middle of a highway, knowing she'd never make it to safety on the other side.

"Chad kind of challenged me to take this trip with a woman I didn't know. My board was making demands." The words rattled from her new husband with the speed of a machine gun.

"So this was all about business?" Amy struggled to swallow the lump in her throat, relieved when it turned to a searing liquid, like tears. Although Mallory reached for her hand, she backed away. "You went on Travel Chums, looking for some poor, stupid woman who would take a trip with a stranger and marry you…because of a bet? To please your board?"

Everything slotted into place. The concourse buckled under her feet.

Mallory reached out again, but she kept retreating. "Not marriage. That wasn't the original plan. Amy, believe me. Everything changed."

"How?" Nothing made sense.

"I met you."

"Goodbye, Mallory." She couldn't get away fast enough. Her entire world was falling apart, and she wanted that to happen in private. Over to the side, Mallory's friends stood like mannequins.

Her steps quickened until she was half running down the concourse toward the restroom sign.

"Amy, slow down. Please, let's talk." His footsteps kept pace.

She stopped and turned to face him. "Let me make one thing clear, Mallory Thornton, if that really is your name. If you don't leave me alone, I will stand right here and sob."

When she pulled away, he stayed in place.

Feeling like a total jackass, Mallory watched Amy disappear into the ladies' room. He'd hurt her—the one thing in the world he never wanted to do.

"Man, I am so sorry." Chad meandered to his side.

Mallory shot him a disgusted look.

"You should have answered your phone. How did I know?" Chad looked so desperate.

"The phone was off. I thought I had time to talk to you in Savannah. Did you have to have the damn key in your hand?"

"Mallory, Chad didn't mean any harm." Mirandah looked from one to the other, disbelief on her face. "But honestly, you two. How do you think that poor woman feels? Y'all should be ashamed."

Mallory groaned. His cousin had meant well. If it weren't for Chad, Mallory would still be barely making it through the day, keeping himself busy with another acquisition so he wouldn't have to face his empty life.

This trip had started as a lark and ended with a marriage that meant everything. "Did ya'll have to bring the car up here? I never want to see the damn thing."

"We didn't bring the car, okay?" Chad scuffed along next to him, Mirandah's heels clicking on the tile. "Thought Mirandah and I would have a couple days in New York, catch some shows. We're all on the same flight back. I just wanted to surprise you. Make the point that you'd won the bet."

"Oh, for God's sake." When was Chad going to grow up?

When was *he* going to grow up? Mallory could kick himself from here to Savannah.

"She'll get over it, Mallory. Women get over stuff all the time."

Behind them, Mirandah laughed.

Mallory turned. "She's the one, Chad. The one."

His cousin's face emptied and then brightened. "You lucky devil."

Chapter 23

Zipping up her green hoodie, Amy shivered while she waited for McKenna and Vanessa. Why did Petersen's Ice Cream Parlor have their air conditioning on in late September? Her friends had pestered her to meet since her return from Italy. She'd put them off. The start of school had been so hectic, and she had no energy. Just a big hole where her heart used to be.

Every day felt like she was slogging through deep water.

But not the sparkling waters of the Bay of Monterosso.

Vanessa and McKenna burst through the entrance, and she waved.

"Hey, waiting long?" McKenna gave her a hug before sliding into the wire-rimmed soda chair next to her.

"How's the happy bride?" Quick air kiss and Vanessa took the seat on Amy's other side.

"I haven't been waiting long, and I'm fine."

Her friends exchanged a look.

"Why are you hiding out? You married Mallory, right?" McKenna looked puzzled.

Vanessa squeezed her hand. "What's up, Amy?"

She hardly had enough breath for a sigh. "Cripes, one week and I marry a man I don't really know…on a cruise ship, no less."

"So romantic." Vanessa's face turned dreamy.

A waitress came and they ordered their usual hot fudge sundaes. Felt like she was just going through the motions. Her friends plied her with questions. The answers opened up a whole world of hurt.

"Oh, honey. Are you sure you're all right?" Vanessa hovered.

"No."

McKenna looked like she might explode any minute. "Can't you fix this?"

"I don't see how." The whole world felt off. Usually she liked her students. The past two weeks she'd wanted to rip their heads off. Great way to start a semester.

"What about Jason? I suppose that doesn't help. Is he still around?" McKenna asked.

One bright light on her horizon. "Jason took a job at another school and Greta followed. Don't know if Glenn had anything to do with that. But, yes. Both gone. That's not the problem."

"So…from what you said over the phone, sounds like maybe you made a mistake," Vanessa reasoned. "I mean, sure, you can probably get an annulment if Mallory flat-out lied to you. But how you feel about him?"

"I love him."

"Okay, then!" McKenna's hands went up. "Now we're getting somewhere."

Vanessa glowed. "That's wonderful, Amy."

"No, that's a problem." She fought the tears bottled up inside. No luck. Thank goodness she'd taken a table back in the corner. The waitress came with their sundaes and scurried away.

Leaning over her whipped cream, Vanessa pinned her with those blue eyes. "Amy, men do stupid things. God knows Alex has. Doesn't mean they don't love you."

Amy sniffled. "Alex loves you. The two of you have talked it through and it's right. A logical progression. Vanessa, we never talked about love. Stupid, huh?"

Scooping up a spoonful of chocolate and whipped cream, Vanessa frowned. "Trust me, it wasn't that easy with Alex. Men aren't goods with words. Wish they were, but a lot of times, they're just not."

"Besides that, Amy, things happened so darn fast for you. One week. Geesh." Surprise and wonder filled McKenna's voice. "I still can't believe we missed your wedding."

"Sorry," Amy whispered.

"Maybe Mallory hadn't processed all that. Maybe he was feeling a lot but couldn't put it into words."

"Nice try, McKenna. Apparently it was about a car. He had a bet with his cousin." Now she had their attention. Quickly, she skimmed over the scene at the New York airport.

"No man gets married because of a car." Vanessa was adamant.

"Mallory Thornton did. And to rub salt in the wound, now he's helping my mother and my sister with their small businesses. I have to hear about him constantly. They adore him."

"Your mother's always been a good judge of people," McKenna managed around the last mouthful of ice cream. "Besides, they could probably use Mallory's help. Isn't he wildly successful?"

"Why aren't you eating, Amy?" Vanessa broke in. "You're thin as a rail."

Amy pushed back from the table. Just looking at the ice cream made her tummy lurch. "I'm on the Broken-Hearted Diet Plan. My stomach's been off and things taste funny."

McKenna's spoon made an annoying metallic squeal as she scraped the sides of the glass. Amy nudged her uneaten sundae toward her friend. "Here, have at it."

"Stop that! You are too thin." Vanessa grabbed the sundae glass and shoved it back to Amy.

"No such thing."

"Look, I think you should talk to the man." Releasing Vanessa's fingers, McKenna dug into Amy's ice cream. She never seemed to worry about her weight.

"We're texting."

"Ah, the personal touch." McKenna's eyebrows rose. "I'm sure you get a lot settled that way."

"Are you getting enough rest?" Vanessa broke in. "You look exhausted."

"Not enough sleep in the world for me." By the end of seventh period every day, Amy wanted to lay her head on her desk and snooze. Usually, students clustered around her with questions. She took them one by one, but every day got harder. "Guess I'm still catching up from that trip."

"Any details about the honeymoon…the one that was but wasn't?" McKenna asked. "I mean besides the fact that you got married. What led up to that?"

So she dragged out the details. Told her best friends how

glorious it had been, from Rapallo to Venice.

By the end, Vanessa had this dreamy look on her face. "Sure beats Disney World. Sounds wonderful. Also sounds like you have some things to work out with Mallory."

How was that going to happen if she didn't speak to him? By the time the three of them said good-bye, Amy was wavering. McKenna gave her the evil eye, and Vanessa had pulled her aside, whispering suggestions that sent Amy into a tailspin. Ten minutes later, she was waiting for the light to change on Harlem when her phone gave the tiny ping indicating a message.

Mallory's text flashed up. "I wish you would answer."

She tossed the phone onto the seat beside her.

When the light changed, she floored it. Dreaming of the Rialto Bridge, she drove under the tracks of the rattling "L" train on its way to downtown Chicago. By the time she got back to her apartment, all she wanted to do was climb into bed and pull the covers over her head. Maybe being in love was exhausting. She didn't recall ever feeling like this. Not with Jason. Not with anyone.

Her world had reverted to black and white. Before entering her apartment building, she'd turned and taken a good look. The street, the cars, even the changing leaves of the trees—everything was black and white. She dragged that sad thought up the stairs behind her, and it followed her to bed.

That week with Mallory the world felt so vibrant. Seeing everything through his eyes had brought a new dimension to her life. In class, they often discussed point of view. The students liked to speculate about how *The Great Gatsby* would be different if told through Daisy's eyes.

She'd loved seeing Italy through Mallory's eyes, even though his comments often led to questions in her mind. He'd been so sweet, with that soft southern accent and his exquisite manners. Blocking him out completely didn't really seem fair. After all, hadn't she kept her own truth from him?

Amy missed him. This went way beyond sex.

"Too tired to talk tonight," she texted back before she drifted off to sleep. "Soon."

"Soon?"

"At last. A light at the end of the freaking tunnel." Mallory stared at the phone in delighted disbelief.

"The tunnel of Amy?"

"Correct, my man." He slapped the phone down next to his soup bowl. Mallory and Chad were sitting in Corleone's, sipping chianti while they wolfed down *pasta fagioli* with a chaser of Italian bread dipped in pesto. His favorite meal but tonight, tasteless. Every bite took another chunk out of his heart.

What would he give to be eating pesto again with Amy back in Monterosso? Anything. Every blessed car lined up in his garage.

"Making any progress?" Chad asked.

"Not really. Well, one text. I've pleaded with both her mother and sister to help me out here. I am in a heapa trouble, Chad. I've been all over hell and half of Georgia trying to think this out."

"Maybe you need a therapist. You've been jumpy as a kerosene cat lately," Chad grumbled.

Rolling his eyes, Mallory took another gulp of chianti.

His cousin set his fork down. "How many times do I have to apologize?"

"It's not your fault. Not really." Mallory pushed the saucer with pesto aside. "I should have explained everything to Amy while we were in Italy. But I just couldn't, Chad. Truth is, I was terrified. For the first time in my life, scared to death."

"Of what?"

He shrugged. "Didn't take long to realize I wanted this woman in my life. I was terrified that she'd run like hell if she ever knew the truth about how I got there."

"You do have it bad." Chad broke off another hunk of bread. "Thought I was supposed to be the best man in your wedding."

"We already did that. This was different." An understatement and Chad's bemused grin told him as much. "I'm dying here. Amy's last text was hopeful. I have to believe that."

"Final call, Mallory. Cameron Fairchild wants that car. Time to fish or cut bait."

He pushed back from the table. "Told you what you can do with that car."

Chad squirmed. "Painful option. All right then. Car goes to Cameron."

As Mallory drove home that evening, he took his usual Bull Street route, passing the squares of Savannah. End of September, but still felt like summer. In Savannah, fall ambled in with studied gentility. He always enjoyed the season's understated arrival. When he reached Forsythe Park, he stopped the Jag. He loved the sight of the moss dripping from the live oaks leading to the fountain. Couples strolled in the soft darkness or cuddled on benches.

Pain cut a swath through Mallory as wide as Sherman's march to the sea. Public displays of affection, or PDA, happening all around the park. He'd always hated it, but Amy had totally changed his mind. Lordy, she'd changed his mind about a lot of things, including marriage.

Approaching his property, Mallory hit the remote. He didn't feel the usual thrill of satisfaction when the gate at his entrance swung open. Driving through the portico, he lowered this window. The gardeners must have been working that day, and the sweet scent of freshly mown grass filled the air. After parking in the garage, he tapped out his password on the keypad to the rear entry and entered the coolness of his climate-controlled mansion.

Nellie always left a light on in the kitchen. Opening the refrigerator, he took out a carton of milk. That wine was wreaking havoc with his stomach. After pouring half a glass, he rooted around in the larder until he found the ginger snaps. Milk and cookies might ease the burning pain that plagued him since his return from Italy. The spicy soup hadn't helped. He hardly knew what he was eating until it took a sharp knife to his insides. Or was this infernal burning in his heart?

Trudging up the wide front staircase, he thought about the couples in Forsythe Park. Damn lucky and they didn't know it. Reaching into the box, he came up with a handful of cookies. Anything to stop this stomach pain.

In the upstairs hallway hung family portraits, including an oil of his mother. Only in her twenties, Anne Thornton exuded girlish charm. Not hard to see why his father had fallen in love with the belle of Atlanta. Owen Thornton had commissioned the painting shortly after Mallory was born, and it had hung in his father's private office at Thornton Enterprises until his death. Portraits of the three of them as a family were also showcased against the green moiré wallpaper. One family grouping always brought a smile. As his mother had told it, Mallory had caused such a ruckus at the sittings that the artist threatened to abandon the project. Finally she allowed the use of photographs as a reference points for her rambunctious little boy.

His parents had treasured that painting, commissioned when Mallory was about three. His father's left hand rested on Mother's shoulder with genuine affection, her right hand clasping his. Romance and passion, that was what his parents had held for each other. One for grand gestures, Owen Thornton had plied Anne with trips and gifts galore. Sure, his father had been driven by the corporation he created, but he'd been madly in love with his wife.

Love.

The floor shuddered, and his box of ginger snaps slipped to the carpet. Earthquake? He grabbed the banister that circled the upper hall. But all was still.

All but his beating heart.

Damnation. He was in love with Amy.

In his mad rush to seal the deal, had he told her?

This might call for a grand gesture.

Chapter 24

Amy sat in her car outside her mother's house. Mom and Aunt Em were expecting her and Caitlin for Sunday dinner. For the past week, she'd done nothing but send text messages to Mallory saying she didn't want to talk to him. The misery of waiting had made her sick.

Truth was, she was too afraid to talk to him. Afraid to hear words like "mistake."

Shoving open the car door, she made it up the steps to the red brick house. Her mother never locked the door on Sundays. The smell of meatloaf curled toward her when Amy entered the living room, and she pressed one hand to her heaving stomach.

"Finally, we've been waiting for you!" Wiping her hands on her apron, Aunt Em bustled out of the kitchen and gave her a good, sound hug. "How you doing, chickadee?"

"Pretty good."

"You don't look it."

"Good to know." Her aunt wanted a smile and Amy gave it to her.

"Dinner in ten minutes. I'm stirring the gravy," her mother's voice sang out. Door still open, Aunt Em peeked over her shoulder. "Looks like Caitlin's right behind you."

Her sister had pulled up behind Amy's car, parking under one of the oaks that bordered the walk. One brisk gust of late September sent dry, red leaves skittering over the sidewalk. Amy would have to come over and help Mom and Aunt Em rake, a task that today seemed impossible. Where was her energy?

"Hello, hello. Sorry I'm late. Kurt can't come. Off to a Bears' game." Unzipping her brown quilted jacket, Caitlin pushed the door closed behind her. "What happened to Italy and warmer weather?"

"Not asking the right person." Amy gave her a hug.

Aunt Em retreated to the kitchen while the two sisters set the table. Amy always laid the plates while Caitlin took care of the silverware.

"Mom tells me you're not answering Mallory's calls."

"Texts only. Just not now, okay?" Had Mallory mentioned the bet to her family? She'd avoided them since her return, but he obviously hadn't. The air felt thick with disapproval.

"But you two are married! How can you not talk to him?"

Amy studied the table. Always the same mistake…since second grade. "The blade faces in, Caitlin."

"Does it matter?"

Caitlin's sigh weighed on Amy. Maybe she was the one just a beat off. Circling the table, she flipped each knife. "Yes. No. Oh, Cait, I don't know anymore!"

Throwing up her hands, she wandered out to the kitchen. Mom's face was flushed from the heat of the stove as she handed Amy the platter of meatloaf circled by browned potatoes. Usually

Amy's favorite, but not tonight.

"How you doing, honey? Haven't had much time to talk to since we got back. Mallory just started right in with us, and it's been so busy."

"He can be like that."

"We're learning about business plans." Aunt Em held the swinging door open for Amy.

"How's that coming?" She couldn't help but smile even though the meaty scent was turning her stomach.

"You'd be surprised. Of course, Mallory's so patient…" Aunt Em's voice took it from there.

Amy nodded. Didn't she know how charming the man from Savannah could be? Sitting at the table in the heart of her family, Amy felt something was missing. She remembered all the meals her mother had served in this room while she was growing up. A time of coming together—that's what each meal had been.

So, why did she feel lonely?

Glenn has just finished the morning's announcements the next day when Al Wesley appeared at the door of room 207. "Time to write in your journals," Amy directed her junior writing class before turning to Al, who taught in the classroom next to hers. First period was his prep period, so what was he doing here? "Hey, what's up?"

She couldn't read her colleague's smile. "Haven't got a clue. Glenn sent me up to get you."

Her heart stuttered. A family emergency? "Is everything all

right?"

"Right as rain." A bear of a man, Al waved his coffee mug and stared down the students who were way more interested in them than in their journals. "Not to worry, okay? Just happened to be passing by and he sent me down. Some paper for you to sign or something. I'll stay here 'til you get back. What's your lesson plan for today?"

"Thesis statements. That'll teach you not to hole up in the lounge during your prep period." She took off, not wanting to inconvenience Al for long. What paper could Glenn have for her?

The second floor hallway was quiet except for Darlene's voice carrying out into the hall as she discussed *Beowulf* with her freshmen. Amy took the stairs down to the main office on the first floor. When she opened the door to the first floor, the strong smell of flowers engulfed her, as heavy as the sweet scents of Rapallo or Venice. Amy's stomach lurched.

Was that really her mother, beaming as she stood next to Aunt Em in the pretty dress she'd bought for her original wedding? A sight for sore eyes in his navy jacket and blue striped shirt, Mallory was flanked by McKenna and Vanessa. Bright-eyed and looking oh, so pleased, McKenna and Vanessa smiled encouragement, while Caitlin grinned. Mallory looked decidedly nervous. From somewhere, a squeezebox played and she was transported. If she closed her eyes, she was back in Italy.

Glenn hovered in his doorway, a look of bemusement on his face. His assistant threw Amy a secret smile before disappearing back into the office.

"What's going on?" Clutching her green sweater around her, Amy gave her head a good shake. She could swear the song played by the musician with dark curly hair was "Return to Me," one of the numbers she'd listened to again and again on her Dean Martin CD since she got back from Italy.

With the endearing smile she'd carried in her heart since Italy, Mallory began to sing, off-key and wonderful. At the end, he sank to one knee while her mother wiped away tears. "Amy, I love you. Be my wife. Return to me, darlin'. I'm begging you."

Her mother and aunt burst into applause. In the commotion that followed, Amy might have been the only one to hear Mallory's words. Gathering her into his arms while her heart brimmed with love and her stomach did a back flip, Mallory told her he'd given up the reins of his company to his cousin. He intended to stay here in Oak Park, helping her family. "As long as it takes for you to know you're my wife."

The idea was crazy, wild and wonderful.

She'd follow him anywhere.

"Yes, yes, but I should tell you something…"

Wearing the smile that had won her heart in that restaurant in Monterosso, he waited.

"Mallory, I have to use the restroom…".

Epilogue

Nine Months Later

Amy stood back to study her handiwork. Cheerful giraffes and mischievous monkeys smiled at her from the green and yellow wallpaper of the nursery. "What do you think?" she asked Caitlin. "Appropriate for a miracle child?"

"I think you should be sitting down." Gently, Caitlin took the wallpaper brush from her sister's hand and nudged her into the white wicker chair they'd found at a flea market. "Look at your ankles. Too much time on your feet."

Amy glanced down and then remembered she hadn't been able to see her ankles for more than two months. Thank goodness school had just ended for the year. She'd lumbered through the last weeks. Resting one hand on her bulging stomach, she smiled. "Gianna likes it."

"What if it's a boy? You wouldn't get the ultrasound," Caitlin scolded. "Everyone at McKenna's shower complained about all the yellow baby clothes."

"I like surprises. That much is certain." Hadn't this pregnancy been the surprise of her life? Mallory's too. The man was over the moon…or the marsh, as he would say

"*Cara*," he'd told her, nuzzling her neck. "I hope we have a little girl. She'll be beautiful, like you."

"You couldn't handle two of me."

"That's more than true, darlin'. It shore 'nuff is." He'd laughed with delight.

After his surprise declaration in the middle of Immaculate

Heart of Mary High School, Mallory had settled in with her in Oak Park. Of course, the small apartment drove him crazy so he'd found this house, not far from her mother. Said he wanted to keep a place in Oak Park anyway, making her family very happy.

After the baby came and things were settled, they would move to Savannah. She felt awed by his mansion that sat in the historical district, but they would be together. When he made short business trips back to Savannah, she felt so lonely. His board had insisted he return to head the company and Mallory had agreed, but on his own terms. She was so proud of him.

Caitlin edged closer, lips curled into a curious smile. "Can I feel? Just one little pat?"

Amy nodded. Throughout the pregnancy, her sister had been a gem. She was the only one who could totally share in the wonder, since only Caitlin knew of Amy's earlier prognosis. According to Amy's new doctor, Logan Sinclair, she'd defied the odds with this unexpected pregnancy.

"McKenna says the head's in position," she murmured. How great was it that one of her best friends was a midwife? Amy's desire to have their baby here, surrounded by friends and family, had Mallory's total support. McKenna would deliver the baby in her water birthing suite down at Montclair Specialty Hospital, where McKenna worked.

Taking one of her sister's hands, she rested it where a foot poked upward. The pregnancy and all the discoveries of the last nine months were still a mystery to her. Vanessa had laughed with delight as Amy's situation unfolded.

"Pregnancy by mistake," Vanessa had teased her at their monthly meeting at Petersen's Ice Cream parlor. "Worked for me."

Now Amy placed one hand carefully over her sister's, and they shared a smile. The baby felt busy today. Then Caitlin went back to work. Heaving herself to her feet, Amy pressed a hand into her aching back. The wallpapering must have stretched muscles she hadn't used in a while.

Her sister began packing up the wallpaper supplies. Mallory had wanted to hire someone to decorate the nursery but Amy has insisted on handling it herself. Caitlin had agreed.

Feeling as if a bowling ball was weighing down her lower stomach, she kicked off her sandals and rubbed her tummy, now very rigid. "Whew, take a nap, Gianna Anne." Mallory had been so pleased when she'd suggested they add his mother's name.

What felt like a cramp caught Amy by surprise, only this was the worst cramp she'd ever had. Wow, she couldn't get her breath.

"You okay?" Caitlin came closer.

Amy waved her away. "Perfectly fine." After all, the baby wasn't due for another two weeks.

Caitlin shook her head. "You're probably hungry. I'll go out and pick up something. Don't mess with the newspapers on the floor. I'll take care of it when I get back. When will Mallory be here from the airport?"

"Any minute now. He landed about an hour ago." After the door slammed behind Caitlin, Amy sat down again in the sunny room. Here she would sing the baby to sleep, read *Good Night Moon*, and plan the first Halloween costume.

This pregnancy had been such a surprise. Apparently Mallory's "vintage supply" of condoms failed and her situation wasn't as dire as her former GYN had predicted. The last months had passed in a glorious blur.

Now she probably needed a nap. First, this room needed cleaning up. Pushing herself up from the chair and ignoring her sister's advice, Amy bent to roll up the papers.

The water left her with a whoosh. Amy stared at the dampened newspapers at her feet. How relieved she was to hear the front door slam.

"Caitlin! Mallory?" Waddling into the living room, Amy took deep breaths.

"Good God, darlin'." Mallory's face drained of color. His bag thumped to the floor.

"Hospital," she groaned.

"Nothing to worry about. I put the address in my rental car's GPS soon as I picked it up."

After gathering her bag, Mallory helped her to his rental car. Curious, the blue car sure looked like an update of their rental in Italy. Totally unlike her car-crazed husband. "Really? Are you kidding me?"

"Humor me. Besides, no one else wanted it."

Once in the car, Amy called McKenna, who would meet them at the hospital. Then she put in a call to Caitlin. Since Mallory had a heavy foot, they were at Montclair in twenty minutes. She'd never seen the Eisenhower fly by so fast. McKenna met them at the door of the ER.

"What were you doing today?" she asked Amy.

"Putting up wallpaper."

McKenna and Mallory both groaned.

In no time at all, Amy was dressed in her sports bra and hospital gown. The water birthing suite on an upper floor of the hospital was small and intimate. Face pale, Mallory helped Amy into the shallow bath.

When McKenna asked Amy to pant, Mallory also puffed out breaths. She grabbed his arm and squeezed so hard he'd probably be bruised for some time. The man never flinched.

Sometime during her labor, a tall good-looking doctor in surgical scrubs and hat entered the birthing suite.

"Dr. Logan?" McKenna greeted him.

He nodded, eyes shifting between Amy and McKenna, who had put her in touch with her new obstetrician just in case complications arose. Sinclair Logan was head of OB/GYN at Montclair. "Everything all right?"

"Fine." McKenna's chin went up. For a second, tension zinged tight in the air. She saw the look that passed between her friend and Dr. Logan.

But that's another story.

The door closed behind Dr. Sinclair when he left.

"What's up between you two?" Amy asked when her contraction had eased.

"Nothing."

Amy didn't believe that for a minute but time to get back to work. The labor picked up as midnight approached. Mallory and

Amy listened to the Italian love songs they'd chosen for their birth plan. McKenna had laughed, saying that was a first.

Suddenly, contractions picked up, coming so fast she could not catch her breath.

Their little girl pushed into the world in record time. Three hard contractions and she catapulted into the water like a sprite, the cord unfurling before McKenna scooped her up. Mallory looked like he might faint, but his pallor was soon replaced by a proud smile.

"How about that, Mrs. Thornton?" he murmured.

Mrs. Thornton. Maybe for the first time, that name felt right.

After a general cleanup with all clinical information duly noted, McKenna nodded to the pediatric nurse, who bundled the infant into a portable bassinette. "Let's get you up to your room. Baby comes too."

Upstairs in the maternity unit, staff buzzed around their little family. Confusion hit a peak when Louise and Aunt Em arrived, along with Vanessa and Caitlin. As evening fell, Caitlin cleared the room and left. After eating some jello, Amy drifted off to sleep. When she awakened in the middle of the night, Mallory was slumped in the chair at the side of her bed, his hand holding hers. Next to him, the baby slept. The whole room smelled powdery and sweet. A rumpled mess, her husband had never looked better.

The baby whimpered in her sleep, and Mallory jerked upright. She'd never seen his eyes open that fast when they were traveling together. Jumping up, he hovered over the bassinette. What a sight. Her heart turned over. Gianna didn't even open her eyes, just fell back to sleep. After tucking the blanket more snugly around the baby, Mallory remained mesmerized. "Damn, have you ever seen anything so amazing? A miracle."

"*You're* amazing."

"So are you, *cara*. So are you." His gaze caught hers, love swirling in their blue depths. How could she ever have doubted this man?

"You should go home," she whispered. "You look exhausted."

Bleary-eyed, he shook his head. When he kissed her, she felt the soft brush of his chin stubble and breathed in his wonderful, familiar scent.

He tightened his hold on her hand. And on her heart.

"Are we your package deal?" she teased.

"Sure are. Italy didn't capture my heart. *You* did, *cara*."

"Did you ever rate your trip on Travel Chums?" she asked after a long, leisurely kiss.

"I'd like to do some quality testing before I issue an official rating."

"I'm pretty particular myself," she whispered, smoothing the collar of his shirt. "Good with details. I could help."

"We may have to be very thorough."

"I'm counting on it. Just give me some time."

"Can't wait 'til we're home. This reminds me of the bed in Florence." Moving with the grace of a southern gentleman, Mallory aligned himself next to her. When had she ever felt this content?

Mallory was right. Sometimes life was just a miracle. Her hold tightened on him. For her, he was home.

THE END

Coming Soon

Her Favorite Hot Doc

A Windy City Romance

If you enjoyed Amy's adventures with Mallory, you might also enjoy McKenna's story. In "Her Favorite Hot Doc," the feisty midwife goes head-to head with Dr. Logan Sinclair, head of the Obstetrics Department and a certified Chicago Hot Doc. The two might hold different perspectives on the needs of their department, but the needs of the heart? Totally on the same page. However, when Logan decides to join Amy for the Midwives in Action trip to Guatemala, McKenna fears it might be the end of their relationship. Or will it be the beginning?

"Sorry I'm late." Sliding in across from him, McKenna pushed back a wave of red hair. Easy to post her in any hallway, and usually Logan avoided her. Not tonight. Cheeks flushed, she always looked like a woman in a hurry. A wave of damp, late spring air rolled over him. Long day, but his fatigue vanished.

"Had a couple of add-ons. You know how that goes. Seeing an extra patient or two late Tuesday can free up my Wednesdays. But then Wednesdays get busy too." Her laugh broke over him like a summer wave on Lake Michigan.

"Not too long ago I didn't have hours on Wednesdays."

"So you were one of those, huh? Probably busy golfing and other fun things."

"How did you guess?" Golf and sailing were his two outlets— sometimes alone, not that he liked it. "But now the schedule is getting too backed up with only the three of us in the group to handle it. We're recruiting. I have a candidate coming in next week." The recruiters better come through for him. The name had sounded familiar, like someone he'd known in high school. "Golf's great exercise. Beats going crazy."

Tilting her head, she narrowed her eyes. "I'd like to see you go crazy."

He sucked in a breath and waved to the waiter, who headed over with a bowl of peanuts. Why did McKenna rattle him like this? "Are you on call?"

"Nope. Selena's got me covered. You?" She wasn't wearing lipstick, but her full lips didn't need any emphasis.

"Gary's on tonight. What would you like to drink?"

"I'll have a beer." She glanced at his lager. "Bud Lite."

"You drink beer?" Most of the women he took out ordered Cosmos.

She had a cute grin. "Not in a sipping mood so bring it on. I'm parched."

"A pitcher please," he told the waiter.

Her delicate eyebrows peaked. "Whoa. A pitcher. You're upping the ante?"

"So, you play poker too, I suppose." McKenna was full of surprises.

"With five brothers I had no choice."

"Warren was telling me that you have a large family."

She frowned. "You were talking about me?"

"Just business. Must be nice to have brothers and sisters."

"Crazy is more like it." Her returning smile held fond memories. By this time the waiter had brought the pitcher, with a mug for McKenna. Logan poured, and she hoisted that frosty mug like a pro. A foam moustache beaded her upper lip and she quickly erased it with the tip of her tongue.

The heat that crackled through his chest and headed lower caught him by surprise.

The music had changed from heavy metal to bluesy jazz. The kind that melted your mind. Maybe the lager was getting to him. Been a long time since he really relaxed. Looking at McKenna's antics with her tongue, muscles he hadn't used in quite a while leapt to life—like a much-needed wake-up call. Strictly a physical reaction.

She leaned forward, as if sharing dark secrets. "It was insane, all those kids. But I wouldn't trade them for the world." Her eyes got this faraway look, like she was remembering boisterous Christmas mornings and graduations when her family cheered wildly as she got her diploma.

Enough of that. "So, I suppose you have tons of nephews and nieces."

"Kirkpatricks reproduce like rabbits. Most of us, anyway." She squeezed both arms around herself.

He shot to his feet. "Air conditioning's too high in here. Take my jacket." Shaking it out, he swung it around her delicate shoulders.

"Thanks, Logan. It was great to get your call," she continued after he'd slid back into the booth. As she bent her head toward him, that mischievous wave of hair fell over one eye. She pushed it back, but too late. For sure, the vampy image would stay with him.

Probably came from not having a life. No personal life, anyway. Tonight, he felt curiously loose and energized. Must be the music. Crunching a fistful of peanuts, he popped one in his mouth and got back on topic.

"As I said on the phone, the rumor is true about the Foundation. They would like to fund an obstetrics project. Warren was asking me for input and I mentioned both the OR renovation or your suggestion of the LDRP."

"That's great, Logan." But she sure didn't sound enthusiastic.

"Warren suggested that we call our groups together, physicians and midwives, and arrive at consensus. Shouldn't take much, right?"

McKenna took a deep gulp of beer, leaving a foamy moustache. "Sounds right. Consensus, huh?" She pursed her lips. Full, naked lips. His mouth went dry.

"He'd like us to present to the Foundation Board in a couple of weeks, so we have to get on this."

One finger traced the upper rim of her mug. Just watching her hand, he felt that light touch on his chest. "Gotta get moving on this one, I guess." She looked to him for agreement.

"Glad you feel that way." His chest still tingled.

"Who should be on the committee?"

She was wondering about a committee and he was wondering if she was seeing anyone. When was the last time he'd felt this distracted? Time to get it together. For a few minutes they talked about staff. "Once we decide on our direction, Marketing will help us tee up the presentation. But we probably won't get to that level of detail at this point. We need a basic model and some numbers to put—"

McKenna reached out and the soft coolness of her palm on his hand silenced him. "Sorry, Logan, but I'm starving. It's been a long day and I forgot to eat lunch."

Great. And here he was babbling on. Grabbing menus, he handed one to her.

As she pored over the listing, his jacket slipped off one of her shoulders. She didn't bother to tug it into place. Reminded him of a robe, worn to the breakfast table before they tumbled back into bed.

How long had it been since he'd thought about anything close to that? Flipping open the menu, he scanned the list. "Good God, you could get atherosclerosis just looking at this menu."

There was that laugh again, robust and earthy. "You are such a hoot." McKenna shook her head as she kept reading. Pad in hand, their waiter arrived.

"Let's see. Think I'll have the Burger Bacado with –" And here she looked up and met the waiter's eyes. He seemed mesmerized by her tawny lashes. Or maybe it was the V neckline of her scrubs. McKenna was generously endowed.

"You have sweet potato fries, right?" she asked. And there was that cute nose crinkle again.

"Yes, Ma'm." The waiter lifted his eyes for one moment and then dove back into her cleavage like he was cramming for a Human Physiology exam.

"Great. I'll have the Burger Bacado and sweet potato fries." She snapped the menu closed and tucked it back behind the napkin dispenser.

With considerably less interest the young man turned to Logan. "I'll have the veggie burger with coleslaw," he said. "Is the slaw fresh every day?"

The waiter blinked. "Yeah, sure. The bags come in every day, I guess."

Right. He wouldn't be eating a lot of that. After the waiter left, the music changed and the panting of Donna Summers cloaked any conversations. *Just what he needed.*

Taking another swig of beer, McKenna leaned forward. "Back to business. How do you plan to reach consensus? Will there be a vote of the committee?"

"Hadn't gotten that far yet." Wouldn't the other clinicians see the logic of what he was suggesting?

The concern in McKenna's eyes let him know that might not happen. He had to regroup. "I'll bring all my research. You might want to do that too. What, too much detail?"

Her brows had lifted and he chuckled. His grandmother often teased him about not seeing the forest for the trees. He didn't want McKenna to think of him that way.

Head tilted, McKenna grew serious. Two little lines bracketed her full lips, as if straining from the luscious weight of her mouth. "Your patients respect your attention to detail. Certainly you know that, Logan. And your empathy."

"Attention to detail." The words felt like a prison sentence. "Guess that about wraps me up."

For a second she just looked at him. "Those are good qualities in medicine. Both staff and patients admire you for that."

Her comment was about the biggest turn-on ever.

"I've been getting up to speed on your fertility clinic," McKenna continued. "You know, just so I can offer it to patients if needed. You bring hope to a lot of women. That's huge."

Usually compliments sounded contrived and left him cold. Hers didn't. "We're recruiting so I can spend more time developing the clinic. You might say it's my passion," he admitted.

"Everyone should have one…passion, that is." Her green eyes burned almost blue.

What was McKenna's passion? Suddenly, he wondered.

Sucking in a slow breath, he was relieved to see their waiter approaching. The scent of grilled burgers reminded him that he was hungry. "Ketchup?" he asked, lifting the red container.

"Yes, please."

After wiping the plastic cylinder with his napkin, he handed it to her. Lifting the top of her hamburger bun, McKenna applied her ketchup with a liberal hand, swirling a red stream over her sweet potato fries with abandon. When it was his turn, he squirted three dots of ketchup onto his veggie burger.

Looking up, he caught her smiling. "What?"

She shook her head. "Nothing." Eyes sparkling, she took a generous bite of her burger and began to chew with slow appreciation. Was that her or Donna Summers groaning? He was toast. Logan reached for his beer.

"You know, I've heard that how a person eats tells you how

they make love. What do you think?" Her glance was all wide-eyed and innocent.

Choking, he spewed droplets of beer onto the table. Grabbing a napkin, he began dabbing. "Well, I really haven't thought about it." Now he could think of nothing else. Had she noticed that he'd edged his coleslaw to the side of his plate?

As she continued to lay out this theory, her voice took on an almost clinical note—as if they were discussing the difference between vaginal delivery versus a C-section. Her fingers dallied with her fries, eyes gauging his response from lowered lashes.

She was playing with him.

Time to turn the tables. "What's your opinion on this, McKenna? Did you come up with anything?" He couldn't keep his eyes off her delicate hands. The way they held a fry to her lips, ran it along its length before devouring it.

Tawny eyelashes fluttering, she gave grave consideration to swirling the next fry in her ketchup. He'd never seen anyone wave a fry that provocatively. "In a sense both our careers deal with human sexuality, wouldn't you say? Obstetrics and gynecology have their roots in sex, right? In your opinion, does our enjoyment of food indicate our enjoyment of, well, other physical sensations?"

He'd lost her with "human sexuality." Head swimming, he waved to the waiter. His thighs zinged as if burned by a laser gone wild.

"I really hadn't thought about it." She was smiling when the waiter arrived. "Water, please."

When had he lost control of this meeting?

Her lips closed over a fry, a small comma of ketchup escaping from one corner of her mouth. But her tongue made short work of that. "You really are outrageous," he breathed.

Good God. Did he say that out loud? Smiling, she continued her sexy, mind-numbing munching, sometimes humming along to the music.

But McKenna didn't seem to know it was sexy. At least, he didn't think she did. That was a turn-on in itself.

The waiter arrived and Logan downed the glass of cold water in three gulps.

"So, tell me about your family," she said, changing the topic. "Siblings?"

"Sadly, no." He easily slipped into words that had served him well through the years. "Only son of Isabel Montclair and William Sinclair. My father, an orthopedic surgeon, suffered an untimely death in a ski accident. By that time, my mother was already on her third husband. Currently she lives in Monte Carlo with a man whose name, I believe, is Guido. Number five."

"Whoa. I am so sorry."

Eyes dropping, he swirled the warm beer coating the bottom of his mug. "Nothing to be sorry about. In many ways I've been very fortunate. My grandmother has been the backbone of our family since my grandfather's death. She's alive and well in River Forest. In her early eighties, she still plays golf." The thought of his lovely, but eccentric, grandmother made him smile.

"Sounds like you two have a great relationship."

"The best. She's a great lady."

"Doesn't she still come to the opening of new units? You know, as widow of our founder?"

"You've done your homework." Not many of the staff realized that he had Montclair blood. "Yes, my grandmother keeps up a family presence."

"And you're divorced?" McKenna continued.

"Yep, five years ago, no children."

But here the Q&A ended. Logan wasn't going to carve out any more personal information. The buzz of his phone was a relief. Just Gary sending a text about one of their patients being admitted. The break bought him time. Logan texted his partner with the necessary information. The return to work matters restored a sense of calm. Not that he didn't enjoy being rattled by McKenna. He just wasn't used to it. Seconds later he took care of the bill, although McKenna had grabbed it first.

"Business expense. For bother of us."

With a shrug, she dropped her hand. After he paid the bill, they headed for the door.

"Thursday okay? Early meeting, say seven or so?" he asked, easing her through the crowd, uncomfortably aware of the press of her curves against his body. "I'll have Tamara check with the other staff members."

"Sure, seven is fine. I'll rally the troops." She was so close that he could smell the onion from her burger. An underlying scent teased him, and he sniffed. Peaches. She smelled like onions and peaches.

Suddenly he was hungry. And not for food.

The evening air bathed his face as he pushed the door open. Logan wanted to jog the three blocks to the lake and dive in. Since it was May, he didn't have to brace against a chilly breeze that often sliced through the tall buildings.

The street lamp set McKenna's hair afire as she threw her head back. "Thanks for dinner, Dr. Sin…"

"Logan."

"Logan." She held the final "n" in his name, and his eyes clung to her lips as she slipped his jacket off and handed it to him.

"Hey, you guys. Small world, huh?" Scott Bullard barreled toward them, his arm around a scrub nurse Logan had seen around the OR. Another hot blonde.

A question burned in Scott's eyes but Logan ignored it. "Business meeting," he threw out.

"Right, me too," Scott tossed back, grabbing the door and his date. "Have fun now, you two."

For a second, McKenna looked stunned. Then she laughed. "Seems like we may have some explaining to do." Obviously, she was a woman who didn't care what other people thought.

"Night, Logan." Her voice carried on the early summer air as she backed away.

"Can I walk you to your car?"

"I lucked out." She pointed to a beige Toyota parked at the curb. "Guy was pulling out when I got here."

"Lucky break." *For me.*

He could stand a lot more meetings like this.

They waved good-bye. Head down, he walked to the parking

255

garage where he always angled his car into a corner on the top floor so no one could scrape his red Porsche. By the time he reached his car, their meeting had replayed in his mind at least four times.

Note: If you would like to be notified when "Her Favorite Hot Doc" is released, please sign up for my newsletter at: www.BarbaraLohrAuthor.com.

About the Author

Barbara Lohr writes contemporary romance, adult as well as New Adult, often with a humorous twist. Her early career included teaching writing and lit to high school juniors and seniors, while also writing theater and book reviews. When her career broadened to advertising and marketing, her love of literature and writing remained. Eventually she published more than two hundred short stories in national magazines. Today she concentrates on longer works with feisty women who take on hunky heroes and life's issues. Barbara lives in the Midwest with her husband and their cat, who insists that he was Heathcliff in another life. In addition to travel, her interests include outwitting the deer that insist on sharing her beloved garden.

For more information on the author and her work, please see:

www.BarbaraLohrAuthor.com

www.facebook.com/Barbaralohrauthor

www.twitter.com/BarbaraJLohr

Acknowledgements

Many thanks to Romance Writers of America and my two local groups, the Ohio Valley RWA and Central Ohio Fiction Writers. Both national and the Ohio writing groups work diligently to advance their writers through the publication process. The loops are also invaluable, addressing writing and publishing issues on a day-to-day basis. On a more personal level, Sandy Loyd and Marcia James, thank you for your sage advice and sense of humor. I look forward to enjoying this journey together. Tonya Kappes, we are all fortunate to have a member who crashes through barriers and never asks permission. Gotta love it, and we do. Thanks to Kim Killion for covers that rock and to Nicole Zoltack for her shrewd editing skills.

For my daughters, Kelly and Shannon, we've shared so much, including a love of great stories, from Judy Blume to Janet Evanovich. I am thrilled to have you as my "advisors." My grandchildren, Bo and Gianna, bring me such joy and will probably appear in quite a few of Mama B's novels. To my husband Ted, words aren't adequate to thank you for your love and support. May we have many more wonderful years together that include trips to Leopold's for ice cream.

Made in the USA
Charleston, SC
28 February 2015